TESTIMONY
Selected Stories

Praise for Jack Pulaski

"Jack Pulaski has his turf, and the talent to work it." —ANDREI CODRESCU

"Get the book and read it. And then shower copies on everyone you know who still enjoys moving his or her eyes from left to right." —SVEN BIRKERTS

"Pulaski has a gift for combining the lyrical with the earthy."
—NY Times Book Review

"Jack Pulaski writes convincingly about so many different cultures it is hard to pigeonhole him. He looks at life through the eyes of Jews, Italians and Puerto Ricans, each change of heart and mind as believable as the one that preceded it." —Chicago Tribune

"Pulaski has the language to capture the moment you are swept up by and into, giving you the clamorous, surreal dream that comes with being alive and knowing it." —Milwaukee Journal

"The writing is dense, sensual, often hilarious and entirely confident; the characters are real, with sights, sounds, and smells crowding the page."
—The Seattle Times

"... each story, each sentence ... are so written; by which I mean that one is constantly aware of, admiring of, awestricken sometimes by the power and variety of language, and by the craft exhibited here ... This is prose as dense, evocative, and multi-referential as poetry." —ALICE BLOOM, Hudson Review

"Mr. Pulaski is a wonderful American storyteller. His real American characters: Russian-Jewish boys, Hispanic girls are us, this nation, from their skin on through to their souls. His tales, his book, the work that is to come, make up an abundance of funny and moving moments on the page that I do not hesitate to call a national treasure." —FREDERICK BUSCH

Also by Jack Pulaski

TESTIMONY
Selected Stories

Jack Pulaski

MADHAT PRESS
CHESHIRE, MASSACHUSETTS

MadHat Press
MadHat Incorporated
PO Box 422, Cheshire, MA 01225

The Library of Congress has assigned
this edition a Control Number of
2025940914

ISBN 978-1-968422-00-4 (paperback)

Words by Jack Pulaski
Cover art: *Jack at Work* by Margarita Cuprill Pulaski
Cover design by F. J. Bergmann
Book design by MadHat Press

www.madhat-press.com

First Printing
Printed in the United States of America

for Margarita Cuprill Pulaski

Table of Contents

Foreword

Jack Pulaski's stories come richly grounded in the realities of "Loisaida" (Lower East Side) and Spanish Harlem, in vibrant Jewish immigrant life in Brighton Beach, and in the experience of a "Jew York" soldier, surviving post-war duty in Korea, and as a college teacher enticed to "trip" with '70s students, fatuous and earnest, with his own enthusiasm for booze, a joint or two, and one mushroom, all these experiences on the edge of gorgeous insanity, invoking the ultimate, perplexing sanity of existence. These stories are crazy and wholesome. Jack's prose and imagination easily claim place with the magical art of Marquez, Allende, Neruda, or Calvino:

> Now the young people I speak to are sweetly adamant. When I first arrived from the city, lugging my suitcase across the meadow, and stumbled onto the nude volleyball game, I had a vision out of H. G. Wells' *Time Machine*. The nude college students floating in the paradisal dusk were the lovely and hapless Eloi, and at any moment, the Morlocks, the devolved industrial masses, the kin I fled, would emerge out of a smoking trench and carry off the beautiful people and make a meal of them. But it's not like that at all. I, who first presented subjects to them, have become the subject. It is possible, they insist, to bring about a world ruled by love rather than money, and my participation requires a confession.

Talk about inviting, agile prose when it is a gray November in the soul!

—Paul Nelson

TESTIMONY

The memory insinuates itself, and again I'm back there, trying to exonerate myself. The hot summer day. The mothers stacked on the tenement stoop. Mama perched on the top step. Pregnant Aunt Zelda, her huge belly resting on her lap, sits close to Mama. She glistens with sweat, mouth gasping, her eyes closed. The other women are distributed below, on the descending steps. Somebody's grandma sits on the middle step fanning herself with a newspaper, nodding yes to everything she hears. Next to the babushka is a very young mother to be, a child herself, who looks frightened. One lady cradles an infant in her arms; another near the pavement reaches down and rocks a baby carriage. Me and my kid brother Josh are trying to hit a shiny new penny with a pink rubber ball. I'm eleven, Josh nine. We stand a half dozen paces apart, facing each other at the borders of the box sketched in chalk on the sidewalk. In the middle of the box is the penny we take turns trying to hit with the pink ball, while each of the women take a turn narrating the travail of childbirth. The woman with the baby in her arms recalls how, in the throes of labor she cursed her husband. The lady rocking the baby carriage says that eventually she couldn't hear herself screaming and wonders if that deafness is in some way related to the amnesia that allows her to long for another child. Stout Mrs. Kozckiewicz, the landlord's wife and janitor, emerges from the cellar having pushed open the large metal doors of the bulkhead built into the sidewalk. She's hauled the last of the cans of trash from the cellar, lined them up at the curb, the brimming garbage cans haloed with buzzing flies. She pauses, wipes sweat from her eyes and says,

1

"Five I got. The first four came two at a time. My husband the landlord says, 'In and out, and boom, you're big as a house.' I don't know whether he's braggin' or complainin'. But just in case, when he gets that look in his eye, I bring out his vodka and that makes him sleepy, thank God." Meager Mrs. Cheechko, who has diminished with the birth of each of her six plump babies, so that her housedress hangs like a shroud over her skeletal body, says of her husband Stanley's mysterious vanishings and appearances, "He comes through the door with the bottle of milk I asked him to get three months ago, and says, 'Hello, heart of my heart. I'm home.' I say to him, 'Drop dead.' He says, 'I'm not in the mood.'" Aunt Zelda exhales in sympathy, puts her hands on her big belly and nudges the weight on to her right thigh. Then, from the summit of the top step, I hear my mother announce, "My Ben was a miracle. He came so quick. I was on a gurney in the corridor of the hospital when he crowned. The nurse said it was the easiest birth she'd ever seen. And when I took him home, what a doll! He nursed, he slept, no problems. My Ben was a dream! But his brother Josh, boy oh boy, then I paid. I was in labor all night. Josh tore me to pieces. And that was only the beginning. When I took him home, he cried, he screamed no matter what. From the minute he was born, I never had a minute's peace. But with my firstborn I got a little lucky," she says, lowering her voice, fearful of being overheard by the demiurge who can only create a conscience through punishment. I squirm hearing myself named in Mama's tribute and know Josh also listens. Maybe, that's why I chased the ball into traffic, dodging the car that almost hit me.

I can still hear Mama shriek; inside the shriek, I'm no longer the blessing that marks my brother curse. But in less than a moment, Mama was on her knees in the gutter weeping, hugging my head to her bosom. Then she stood up, looked in the direction of the car that hadn't stopped, and in Yiddish wished cholera on the driver. In the same breath she recapitulated in a scream the event that had hardly passed and was already a legend, grabbed a handful of my hair, yanked me onto the sidewalk and remonstrated against heaven, "Just like his father, he'll put me early in my grave. God Almighty, he scared me out of ten years of my life." And with her free hand smacked me again and again, while her other hand clutched the hair on top of my head, as she pulled me up the steps. The women sitting on the stoop moved to the right and the left to make a clear path. Aunt Zelda called to her sister, "Don't aggravate yourself." Josh trailed behind me and slipped the penny in my back pocket.

THE MATINEE

In my sleep I saw my head resting on the Himalayas of Bubbeh's breasts. My waking leached from dreaming pictographs, coating my tongue with the residue of the language I'd lost. Clearing my throat, dredging spit as for a gut-bucket serenade, the fish fell out of my mouth. I approximated the sounds of words I'd once spoken. The large, wriggling flounder wrapped in damp newspaper, scrolled in Hebrew, the pulsing of the flounder's gills swelled Aleph Beth, and I ran with the fish tucked under my arm. I weaved between pedestrians. Bubbeh charged ahead of me, multitudes fell away before her, like Moses parting the waters; water waiting in the bathtub in her kitchen where I could play with the fish.

My shadow tailed Bubbeh. She negotiated the pavement like the pitching deck in steerage. Having left the city market where I got the fish that now resided in my belly—except for the fish's skeleton that Bubbeh had extracted and set on a plate, alongside the head and tail she'd lopped off—this time we made our way down Broadway and I held a twine-leash at the end of which waddled a duck. Because I said I wanted one. With Bubbeh there were no impediments to my wishes.

The uniformed official emerged from the crowd and marched past a man with the saddest face I'd ever seen. The man with the sad wracked face had signboards hanging from his shoulders displaying a menu with a picture of a steaming bowl of soup. The official maneuvered around a mother pushing a baby carriage. He might have been a cop, or a representative of the sanitation department in mufti. The man with the military bearing placed himself in front of us. He said something to Bubbeh in an English whose cadenced syllables had the resonance of a harp. He was tall, Bubbeh short but monumental sideways. She'd almost plowed into him. She smiled at the musicality of his voice. I sensed his displeasure at whatever it was that undermined his authority. Again he spoke. Bubbeh began to understand. She, not yet a *citizenya*, was law-abiding; she'd feared deportation during the Palmer Raids because her son, Ruben the criminal, beat people up for money. But the deportees were members of the Amalgamated Clothing Workers, the International Ladies Garment Workers and Wobblies. Ruben—Ruby in the street—was only an unkosher capitalist, and that didn't warrant banishment from America.

Later, through years of recitations, I heard from my mother and aunts how Bubbeh had beaten Uncle Ruby when she found out that the money he brought into the house was in payment for beating people up outside of the ring, as well as inside, a trade she wouldn't honor in any case. My mother and her sisters hung on Bubbeh's arms, begging, "Please Mama, stop! You're going to kill him." The blood ran down the side of Uncle Ruby's head. "Mama, please stop, you'll kill him." And Bubbeh, wielding the frying pan said, "Yeah, either I'll make a mensch of him, or I'll kill him."

Despite the requirements of Uncle Ruby's employment (on behalf of Shiv, a.k.a. Baron Slechtman, collecting protection payments) Ruby was a neighborhood hero. His picture was in the paper. Everyone was talking, "Soon a contender." He'd never lost a fight in the ring, and he considered that being out on his feet, blood blurring his vision while Bubbeh knocked him around the kitchen, was a T.K.O. in her favor. Bubbeh belted him, his hands moved only to fend off the words, "Bum!" "Thief!" Unlike in the ring, he didn't move from side to side but staggered straight back. Bubbeh loaded up and whacked him.

Ruby grew from neighborhood hero to local deity. He was the Israelite army defending the immigrant Jewish community against the Wops, Micks, and Polacks. He attained something, a quality of being nearly commensurate with menschhood.

It wasn't achieved through what Bubbeh attempted to pound into his head, but because he fell in love with a horse. It began with a delinquency, when he was twelve, three years before he began to fight pro, and four years before he went to work for the Baron.

Everyone knew everything. The toilets in the hall, windows open or closed, the tenements couldn't house secrets or curtail rampant influenza and tuberculosis.

My mother said Ruby was eleven when it happened, Aunt Tessie said he was twelve. The other five sisters supported the estimate of one or the other, but the permutations of the story didn't change in its essentials except for how each teller of the tale declaimed her innocence: the powerlessness to rescue her mother from working herself to death. There would be lifetimes of testifying to what had made it impossible to forestall Bubbeh dying in a charity ward, old at fifty. The declamations were reprised at each gravesite as my aunts passed away; sometimes too, at weddings and bar mitzvahs where grief and joy cooked up blood pressure leading to stroke and heart attack.

I was at the unveiling of Bubbeh's memorial stone, replacing the modest stone set up in hard times. I was ten and still susceptible to the wailing. I bore witness to the drama which resulted in Aunt Esther's first stroke, slurring her speech and leaving her gimpy, and Aunt Sophie's aneurysm making her forgetful about household routine. Aunt Sophie died a year later.

But as I matriculate in the language of ghosts I hear the guttural sounds, pith, and ruthless wit, an expressiveness that transfigures toil, loving, living, and dying into opera, and has hammered my idiom, how I think and speak, ostensibly in English.

A policeman came to the door to inquire whether Ruby, who was eleven, might assist in finding a horse and wagon that had disappeared. "The onion-and-potato peddler," the policeman said, "depended on the animal and wagon for his livelihood, the horse especially." Ruby's sisters, half of them shoeless, and in their homemade dresses ran into corners and translated for the courteous policeman to Bubbeh. I imagine Bubbeh's bosom trembling as she howled, "*A shande! Mein zin a gonif!*" The policeman quickly surveyed the orange crates serving as chairs, the coal-less stove, and the seven hungry girls trying to hide from his sight and concluded that Bubbeh was a widow. He was essentially correct. Zayde, in crossing the ocean had been turned into a specter. He prayed and studied but was otherwise unemployable. He recognized his children as part of humanity at large, any problems connected to these offspring was woman's work. His only complaint was that on those occasions when he loosened his belt buckle, his wife immediately became pregnant. (*"Shvenget! Nokh a Mol!"*) From time to time, provoked by the outrages of the man-made world, Bubbeh would remind Zayde that he was complicit in pumping up her belly. Then, in vain, Zayde's pride brought color to his cheeks.

There was a scarcity of shoes. When Bubbeh had to leave for work at the commercial laundry and her carpet slippers had walked off on their own, Bubbeh borrowed Zayde's shoes. Whatever the Jewish aversion for idolatry, Zayde's shoes were damned near objects of worship. It was my Aunt Tessie's job to shine them. Bubbeh was forbidden to wear Zayde's shoes. She sneaked when she needed to wear them and swore the children to secrecy.

Bubbeh's life remained a struggle but she had acquired a bed.

Because the warfare between my parents was constant and terrible, and my mother wanted to spare me as much as possible, she allowed me to walk the one block south, to Bubbeh's house. From the age of six on, I made my way there on my own.

If Zayde was in bed with us, I hardly knew he was there. I pressed myself against Bubbeh. When I was in the first grade Bubbeh and I cuddled in bed and read from the same primer. We laughed and struggled to recognize the words and Bubbeh, never increasing her English vocabulary beyond my first-grade primer, didn't venture to get her second papers, and never became a *citizenya*.

Once I wandered into the bedroom and saw my grandfather lying on his belly, naked, little glass cups barnacled all over his back. Bubbeh would lift one at a time and leave a constellation of little bruised suns on Zayde's back.

My mother and Aunt Tessie agreed that it was the same policeman who came to the house the second time. Aunt Zelda, Aunt Esther, Aunt Sophie, Aunt Leah, and Aunt Ruthie, said no, it was a different policeman. But they all agreed that he was patient. "What happened,

Ruby?" the policeman asked. "I found it," said Ruby. "Where?" the policeman asked, "did you find the horse and wagon?" Ruby couldn't explain. The policeman heard a note of complaint in Ruby's voice, some symptom of complicated feeling.

The inhabitants of the neighborhood gossiped Ruby into legend long before he suspected that his being in thrall to a horse was love, and love might not have made him a mensch, but the concomitant symptoms were kindness, devotion, and confusion.

My mother and aunts' story telling is unrelenting and minimally cathartic. I work at reconciling the variations in the stories. The nuances in their telling and pleading spawns telling and pleading. I'm not sure it is necessary to know why these stories have claimed me.

When Ruby was eleven, Bubbeh went to work in the commercial laundry where the women at the tubs and machines had to ask permission to use the toilet. The day's work could last twelve to fourteen hours. The women were not allowed to leave the shop, but their children could bring jars of water and things to eat. Work was not interrupted. Bubbeh took pride in never having fainted.

Rivke the next to oldest, born in Odessa, was taken in the influenza pandemic before her sixteenth birthday. When Rivke was fourteen she'd caught the eye of a gangster. At that time Bubbeh generated income by washing corpses for burial and running a kiosk, where she sold cigarettes for a penny a piece, pretzel sticks two for a penny, and glasses of seltzer, two cents plain. Her working capital never exceeded a dollar and fifty cents. Beautiful Rivke helped out at the kiosk. The sharply dressed dandy stopped at the kiosk a couple of times to buy pretzels that he gave to kids running around the street. He eschewed Yiddish and spoke in Russian. He wore a dark blue overcoat and black bowler hat; his cordial manner and posture exuded a sense of prosperity intrinsic to his destiny. He engaged Bubbeh in conversation, switching from Ukrainian dialect to Yiddish, as if bestowing an endowment he'd grant to only the very special few. His effort not to stare at Rivke was detectable. Halfway down the street, a black, hearse-like automobile was parked at the curb. Bubbeh identified it as a gangster's coach.

The next time the impeccably groomed landsman came to the kiosk, he asked for a pack of cigarettes, Bubbeh's entire stock. Rivke was startled by the extravagant purchase. The gangster's oblique glance surveilled Rivke. Bubbeh studied the gangster and placed the pack of cigarettes on the counter. He picked up the cigarettes and placed a ten-dollar bill on the counter. Rivke stared at the princely sum. The cigar box contained, in coins, one dollar and seventeen cents. Bubbeh said to the gangster, in the language that lurked in my aunts' dreams, as Yiddish lurks in mine, that she couldn't make change for a ten-dollar bill. He made a show of digging in his pockets, extracting wads of currency, but couldn't find anything smaller than a ten. He smiled, shrugged, and turned his head toward the hearse-like vehicle. If Rivke would walk the short distance to the car he was sure his colleague could change the ten for singles. Bubbeh's eyes locked on his. Girls had disappeared from the neighborhood, this part of the city a preserve for such enterprise; the police turned a blind eye. Bubbeh rested the palm of one hand below Rivke's heart, shoved her into a corner, and with her other hand reached down into a pail that held a cake of ice, and the ice pick she used to chip the ice to chill glasses of seltzer water. The ice pick in Bubbeh's fist, she measured the distance to the landsman' throat. He backed away from the kiosk's oblong window. He claimed innocence; this was a misunderstanding. Bubbeh extending one arm kept the ice pick in the vicinity of his face. She hoisted one leg over the counter and climbed out into the street. He who had laid claim to being a neighbor in the old country was no longer smiling. He backed away toward the car, a pistol in his hand. Bubbeh kept coming. She identified him, shouting to mothers congregated on stoops, milk boxes, gathered around the fruit and vegetable pushcarts. She shouted in Yiddish, Russian, and Polish, "Whore master!" The pimp turned and sprinted for the car. Bubbeh chased after him. Women ran from the stoops, and pushcarts. Bubbeh chased the pimp. A horde of mothers ran in her wake. The pimp jumped onto the running board of the car. The vehicle sped off. Bubbeh and the gang of mothers chased after the car for the length of the block.

For Bubbeh, this was one skirmish in a long day. The event, which was told again and again and again until my aunts became curators of the myth, the event itself had an immediate and practical civic effect. The fruit and vegetable vendors, the tailor shop, the grocery, Bubbeh at the kiosk, all would continue to pay their twenty-five cents a week protection money, but the pimps would no longer browse the street to replenish their houses. The mothers were alerted. And it became known, regarding this business, Bubbeh's street was just too much trouble. Bubbeh, like Ruby, had a preeminence in the street. And Bubbeh too would have trouble with the police. Although she managed to keep the young Ruby out of jail, she couldn't do the same for herself.

Ruby was eleven when he was sent to the principal's office for misbehaving in the classroom. The principal removed the leather belt that circumscribed his belly, raised the belt above his head to administer the prescribed number of strokes for Ruby's offense, and Ruby beat him up. The principal required medical attention.

With the aid of a social worker—an uptown young German-Jewish woman of formidable dignity who could speak Yiddish—Bubbeh pleaded, begged, and bargained to keep Ruby out of reform school. She knew her Ruby. If he were caught up in the penal system, given his relationship to authority, any authority, his chances of getting out were minimal. It was more likely that Ruby would kill someone or be killed himself.

Finally the matter was settled: eleven-year-old Ruby left school for good. When they got home Bubbeh smacked Ruby's face. He regarded the blow as a rhetorical flourish. The ringing in his ears diminished with sundown.

Eventually, Ruby would go to jail for a year and a day, as it was a felony for Ruby to use his fists outside of the ring. The man Ruby damaged had been mistreating a horse.

The junk dealer who would be subject to dizzy spells for the rest of his life had a reputation as a mild man. He'd never lifted a hand to his wife or children. To alert customers and assuage the tribulations of his life he beat, furiously, the bell suspended from an L-shaped wooden frame attached to his seat in the wagon. Customers approached to sell buckets without bottoms, rusted wash boards, basins, broken knives, all manner of metal debris. The junk man maneuvering his horse and wagon through the traffic of cars, trolley cars, vendors pushing pushcarts, would in the misery of his life beat his horse with a whip to purge his anger and retain a tenderness for God and the human race. When in the by and by, Ruby became wealthy, he provided Yosip the Junkman with a lifelong stipend, not only because he had injured him, but because Yosip would also introduce Ruby to the scrap-metal business which became the basis of Ruby's fortune.

Despite Bubbeh's well-founded concern, Ruby got through his prison term well enough, but with a greater aversion for human creatures. Upon release Ruby declined the Baron's offer of continued employment. They remained cordial. Ruby apprenticed himself to a farrier, and Bubbeh was arrested for participating in a rally supporting Margaret Sanger. Ruby took to the trade just as horses and wagons were disappearing from the city streets. Pounding steel on an anvil, sparks exploding from his hammer, in the terrific heat the molten U-shaped plates took form, and no one ever fitted a shoe to a horse with such care, with such powerful caresses.

Ruby hoisted the animal as needed and made loving sounds. I remember the sounds Uncle Ruby made at weddings. He would play the two sticks splayed between the fingers of each hand, beating the sticks on his knees, head, and chairs, compounding complex rhythms, the sticks whirring into invisibility; he did the same with spoons, the acoustics ringing a different song. He played the harmonica, and he could tap-dance. He wouldn't, or couldn't talk much, but he could dance. The nimble bear of a man beating music from the floor with his feet, the syncopation wrung joy from my aunts and uncles, who gasped as Ruby's feet flew, the great bulk of him hovering just above the floor.

When the Sanger clinics were set up in Brooklyn, Bubbeh took each of her grown daughters to receive counsel on birth control, and instruction on the correct insertion of the contraceptive pessary. As each married daughter gave birth Bubbeh would arrive shortly after labor to say, "Well, how did you like it? Don't forget. One is enough, two is plenty. A woman shouldn't make soldiers for the Czar!" My aunts repeated to their daughters, "Don't make soldiers for the Czar!"

The injunction has remained in the family. My mother in the early stages of Alzheimer's disease, at the point when long-term memory urgently disgorged itself, shouted at a young pregnant, Portuguese mother (three little ones trailing the mother down the hallway), "Don't make soldiers for the Czar!" The teenage mother was baffled by her elderly neighbor, who shouted the strange injunction at her; until my mother grasping each recalcitrant phrase, each fleeing word, willed coherence and explained to the girl, "Don't make soldiers for the Czar!" The Portuguese girl didn't hear Czar, but cigar, which she associated with her husband, and she understood.

Bubbeh spent two days in jail for her participation in the rally in support of Margaret Sanger. My mother and Aunt Tessie recall that there weren't any coins in the cigar box and they tried to fill up on the stock of pretzels and soda water. It made them sick. Ruby was at the farrier's hammering in a shower of sparks. He stepped out of the blistering rain to stand eye to eye with a mare. The mare's nostrils flaring, Ruby's nostrils flared, they picked up the same scent, shared a way of knowing.

As best as Aunt Tessie and my mother can recall, on the days Bubbeh failed to provide a meal, Zayde felt no hunger.

The consensus of my mother and aunts is that Bubbeh had fifteen pregnancies. One of Ruby's brothers was stillborn, another died after two weeks, another went with Rivke during the influenza pandemic. Bubbeh also had a couple of miscarriages and an abortion. The greatest injury my mother sustained was the knowledge that Bubbeh, desperate, considered giving her away for adoption to a rich lady uptown, who wanted an elder sister companion for her younger adopted daughter. Bubbeh reckoned that whatever her industry, she couldn't feed all her children. My mother, Molly, was well-spoken, the most charming storyteller, but in Bubbeh's estimation, my mother's plain looks didn't make her a promising marriage prospect. Bubbeh worried constantly about how she'd marry off so many daughters without dowries. As often as she was told dowries weren't the custom in America, she was incapable of believing it. In any case the arrangement that had seemed certain fell through and Mother wasn't given away. From that time on, my mother was acutely aware that she was fair-skinned and had reddish hair, while her sisters were dark and had black hair; and despite male attention, and any evidence to the contrary, believed herself homely. The image she spied in the mirror conveyed something sour she couldn't expunge or cover with cosmetics.

The eldest son Ezra's name came down from the scribe and prophet. In spite of Ezra's living until he was twenty-two, he was mentioned obliquely, as when Bubbeh traveled upstate to visit him. The stigma of the sanatorium was more powerful than the notoriety of Sing Sing, where Ruby did his time. Tuberculosis warranted shunning as death was borne on the air, breathing a hemorrhage, the consumptive and his family always a suspect contagion. But the legend of Ruby's invincibility in a fight was community property and helped obscure the memory of Ezra in the neighborhood. When Bubbeh set out to visit Ezra, she did it discreetly. Only the family knew where she had gone.

Bubbeh got a job as a janitor in a tenement with a coal furnace. The job didn't carry a salary, but did provide a rent-free apartment on the fifth floor. Bubbeh shoveled coal into the furnace, hauled trash cans out of the basement. She washed the five flights of stairs and landings on her hands and knees and sustained her employment at the laundry. When a corpse needed washing the Rabbi notified her. My aunts took turns maintaining the kiosk. Still, despite Bubbeh's enterprise, there were hungry days. However stealthily Bubbeh made her journey to visit Ezra at the sanatorium, she appropriated whatever money there was, blatantly, and wouldn't tolerate any argument or pleading to the contrary; as far as she was concerned Ezra would have, in his young, short life, luxuries. Fancy pajamas, a bathrobe like an emperor's coronation gown, fur-lined slippers, books, pencils, crayons, and paper, (Ezra loved to draw and scribbled Yiddish verse). Also caviar, and linen handkerchiefs to cough blood into. When Ezra died, the staff burned his drawings, books, pages of verse, and garments, fire being the most trustworthy hygiene. My aunts maintained, Bubbeh always favored Ezra, even before he'd contracted tuberculosis. If Ezra had represented a refinement too good for this world, Ruby represented to Bubbeh all the barbarities of the new world.

Bubbeh couldn't forget that Ezra was one of the charity cases taken in at the sanatorium, and she slipped coins into the pockets of the white-coated attendants in the hope that the care given to Ezra might be as diligent as that given to wealthy patients.

The aftertaste of hunger could never be assuaged and when the time of plenty arrived at last, gluttony became an expression of filial piety. The children's grievances were expressed as comedy only when my aunts were grown. Telling it at a plentiful table they laughed and convulsed. Ruby didn't laugh, when Aunt Esther recalled the day they realized they were eating the pigeons Ruby had been keeping in a coop on the roof. He loved the birds almost as much as he loved the horses. When Bubbeh confirmed that their mouths were full of the birds he loved, Ruby swallowed, then cried for the second and last time in his life.

From all that couldn't help but be revealed, as my aging aunts discussed their failing bodies, inventoried their aches and pains, ridiculed inadequate medicines, they also gossiped about their marriages. None were happy, a few were resigned and almost content, and a couple tolerable. The union of my parents was a misery. The marriages of her sisters were unhappy for every reason but want.

Many of the marriages, if not arranged by Bubbeh, were strenuously promoted by her. Aunt Tessie, not married until she was eighteen, was considered in danger of being an old maid. Aunt Esther, a beauty with a predilection for nineteenth-century Russian literature, was courted by Sammy the grocer's son. Sammy's family, Bubbeh reminded Esther, was well-off. The grocery was a thriving business, no one in Sammy's family was likely to go hungry with shelves of food near at hand. Also, the Berkowitzes owned a two-family house and every summer they took a bungalow in Coney Island.

Bubbeh didn't need to say that such a marriage might also be a resource for Esther's sisters, an auspicious first step to a better life for all. Esther said she felt nothing for Sammy, despite his attentiveness, industry, and his oddly emotionless confession that Esther's beauty had affected him more powerfully than anything else in life, and that he couldn't imagine denying her anything. Esther was put off by all she imagined Sammy could never imagine. Bubbeh countered, saying that he was quiet, serious, and not altogether ugly; he would provide a fully furnished apartment of Esther's choosing, in a more desirable neighborhood, and he'd promised to help Esther's sisters. Bubbeh argued that there was something wanton in denying such devotion. What were a woman's options? Hadn't she herself married out of some romantic impulse she'd never understood, mistaking Zayde's unworldliness for something lofty that must inevitably enhance love on earth? Bubbeh swore that she hadn't any inkling that in marrying Zayde she'd enlisted to serve the man's reputed genius, so that he might derive sublimity's true existence through mathematical and Cabalistic proofs, barely noticing her children were hungry, and, to make his periodic earthly connection, climb on her (as this too was her duty). Sammy, whatever he couldn't imagine, could provide, and had promised to insure an easier life for Esther. That, Bubbeh said, was the true beginning of marriage.

Esther returned from her honeymoon in the Catskills weeping. She told her mother that Sammy had been kind, patient, and the marriage hadn't been consummated. Sammy, Esther cried, was a soulless materialist and she couldn't bear his touch. She begged Bubbeh, asked if the marriage might be annulled. Esther said she couldn't return to him. Bubbeh commiserated, and she said that Sammy "Pischer," however puny his soul would always dote on her, and as for the bed, Esther should close her eyes and dream what her children's lives could be. With the exception of Mother and Aunt Tessie, Esther's sisters gave the same advice. After a week, Esther returned to Sammy.

Bubbeh paused, looked over her shoulder. I stood with the twine-leash in my hand and watched my duck waddle. The avenue was crowded, people hurriedly side stepping the quacking duck. My sixth birthday was drawing near and Bubbeh had promised a surprise. I wondered whether it would be a cake, or one of the wonderful hats she could fold out of newspaper. The uniformed official from the sanitation department who'd placed himself in front of Bubbeh went on and on about some law we were breaking because of my strolling on a city street with a duck. He'd raised his voice, as if shouting would make Bubbeh understand. Finally, she did understand: the official was presuming authority that allowed him to interfere with her grandson's activity. She said something that sounded like, "Not you biz-nyess," and with one arm swept the official into the passing crowd.

It was a warm summer night. The duck, I knew, would soon be a meal (and I felt no remorse at the prospect, as I was completely taken by the delights and transformations that flowed from Bubbeh's hand). The duck was tethered to a rail on the fire escape, where I would sleep the night. The mattress, pillows, and blanket made a comfortable bed. There were wooden cheese boxes with morning glories all around me. Perched five stories above the street in the cocoon Bubbeh had made I floated in the dark, watched the stars, listened to the melancholic sound vessels hooted from the East River, and opened my mouth as Bubbeh fed me figs.

Bubbeh's present for my sixth birthday was something completely new. It yielded wonders in another darkness, fantastic as anything I saw dreaming on the fire escape. Occasionally it occurred to me that I'd been away from home for some time. There had been an unexpected silence there, more frightening than the curses my mother and father hurled at one another, the silence threatening to explode into something more awful.

Bubbeh took me by the hand. The duck remained on the fire escape. Bubbeh pointed to the morning glories, the flowers opening with the light. We made our way through the streets. Bubbeh pointed to various stores, a furniture factory at a corner where we turned, pinched her nostrils as we walked the thoroughfare of slaughterhouses, past the gas works, and a store front where gypsies lived; there were two large windows with a purple door in between. On one window there was a giant painted eye, and some writing with a number of words I recognized; I assumed the writing was an invitation. On the other window the enormous palm of a hand. I wondered why the gypsy families made their homes in stores rather than apartments. Bubbeh pointed out the gypsy residence as a landmark. She guided me in the language of ghosts, and the pictographs her hands shaped in the air.

Unlike Hansel and Gretel I was meant to find my way home. She caressed the top of my head and in language of ghosts blessed my brain.

Outside the movie theatre, standing near the ticket booth she put coins in my hand. I counted fourteen cents. She was delighted with my ability to compute and kissed me. I could tell time, and this also seemed miraculous to Bubbeh and as she found it miraculous, so did I. At her urging I bought my ticket.

In the lobby I walked up an incline, inhaling perfume thick and sweet as candy. Bubbeh summoned the manager who was also the ticket taker. He must have been a landsman because she spoke to him in Russian. I surmised that she'd said, "This is my grandson; make sure no one bothers him." He nodded his head and dropped the torn ticket into a tall black box. The landsman was wearing a suit, shirt, and tie bloated and wrinkled, as though he'd just been retrieved from the ocean. The movement of his hands, his head, was mechanical. He had a lost look, reminiscent of Zayde as he took and tore tickets the movie patrons gave him, most of them children and adolescents.

The arches of red, yellow and blue light bulbs, surrounding the colored posters on the walls of the narrow lobby on either side of me, pulled my head to the right and left as I walked up the incline of the lobby. A cowboy in a ten-gallon hat sitting on a rearing stallion brandished six-shooters, a giant gorilla sat on top of a skyscraper with a screaming girl in the palm of his hand, a man in a cape with mad, gleeful eyes and a smile of brilliant teeth thrust a sword toward the sky: I glimpsed a sinking ship, the panorama of a burning city. I clutched the soiled comic book the lady in the ticket booth had given me. She'd said that every boy and girl who bought a ticket before noon would get a free comic book.

Bubbeh grasped the elbow of the manager and pulled him along. They accompanied me to my seat. She kissed me, gave me a brown paper bag containing a slice of pumpernickel smeared with chicken fat, a smaller bag inside the bigger bag with raisins, and a jar of tea, and two cents for candy. She hugged me. I knew she believed in my ability to find my way back to her house. I wasn't afraid.

I sat in the teeming dusk and watched children hatching in the dark. In front of me, in the distance, loomed the great surface of a screen, dim and pocked as the mountains of the moon. Down to the left of the screen was a concession stand attended by a shadow. Sweet smells drifted from the stand, and from somewhere behind the stand the smell of frying potatoes, sauerkraut, and hot dogs. My seat sprung coils of hairy stuff. Beams of light fell through the roof, illuminating dust motes. Looking up toward the roof I could see clusters of bubbles swelling and trembling. Rain fell soaking the head of a man as derelict-looking as the one I'd seen on Broadway with the great sandwich board hanging from his shoulders, advertising soup. He snored. I wondered whether he'd bought a ticket to come in and sleep, or if, as an act of charity, the manager had let him in to snooze in the back row where his smell could be washed away by the rain that fell through the ceiling.

The dark filled up, became riotous. The great tabula rasa at the end of a long smoking cone of light teemed with stampeding cattle, mooing in the swirling dust; a cowboy on a magnificent white stallion galloped after a wagon dragged by a sextet of berserk horses; a girl in the careening wagon screamed. The cowboy plucked the girl from the wagon and sat her on his saddle as the wagon plunged over a cliff. The cheers in the theatre drowned out the sound of the cattle. A vendor made his way up the aisle hawking ice cream. Another hawked hot dogs. Their voices, ballooned and gravelly could be heard above the bedlam. I followed the cone of light down to the concession to the left of the of the screen, saw the silhouette of my head darken the chest of Johnny Mack Brown's stallion. I purchased two sticks of licorice for a penny, and for the other penny a thin filament of paper with pink sugar drops on it.

When I'd learned Johnny Mack Brown's name, I wanted his name and wanted to be him.

I watched Tarzan wrestle a crocodile. All the sounds of a jungle rose, bird calls trilled in the dark, elephants trumpeted, an amphibian roar swallowed the hours and I munched the pumpernickel smeared with chicken fat. Tarzan strangled the crocodile. I coughed, breadcrumbs caught in my throat. My eyes teared. I took the last swallow of tea. My head jerked sideways and I saw a beautiful, bandana-ed gypsy lady sitting next to me, smoking her pipe and bouncing an infant on her lap.

The baby began to cry. The gypsy lady opened her blouse and popped her breast into the baby's mouth. I put a raisin on my tongue. The baby sucked. My vision listed toward the gravitational force of the milk-filled moon; the baby sucked; I swallowed the raisin. The gypsy woman took her breast from the baby's mouth, the plum-colored nipple pointing at my nose. She smiled as if to offer me a sip. I choked.

Like everyone else, I forgot the name of the movie house; it was simply known as "The Dump". By the time I was fourteen the Puerto Rican kids called it "*El Meaito,*" I asked my pal Hector Perez what that meant. He said, "A place where one may piss."

Faithful, wedded to years of matinees, Hector and I attended every Saturday. The ambrosial stink was the same. Saturday morning in the lobby, Bubbeh's landsman was still there (Bubbeh four years gone); the ticket taker, no older than he'd been the first time I saw him, still looking as though he'd just been fished from the sea, tore the admission tickets in half.

In the semi-dark of the theatre, Hector and I and the packed audience waited for the show to start. Hector explained to the boy sitting behind him, who sneezed on his ear and refused to step outside, "Either you got valor or you a piece of shit." He had to shout to be heard over the stamping feet, clapping, and whistling.

The theatre darkened. There was thunder outside, and thunder inside. On the screen the Wolf Man stalked through the mist. Someone's hat was launched, a shadow lobbed again and again with cheers, the shape of some attenuated flying thing, wingless, passed through the projector's cone of light just in front of the Wolf Man's gnashing teeth. The Wolf Man menaced a young woman. Hector shouted encouragement and genuflected. Wolf Man's furry brow metamorphosed with the waning of the moon to suffering, thoughtful flesh. The young woman escaped. I thought of my mother and father, each fearful of the other in their ordained madness.

Meanwhile, large, chaste, bumbling Lon Chaney Jr., subject to the merciless moon, begged to be locked up, rage and carnage some deity's test of his innocence. The howl came from the balcony. "You pissed on my shoes! You pissed on my shoes and you say you're sorry?" The sound of the scuffle coincided with the most pious moment, Wolf Man dying into human form, the face contrite, at rest, a rapture of peace and death. Between the main features we saw a Three Stooges comedy. I watched the Stooges bang one another over the head with hammers, heard the buffo tune of perpetual calamity, the mocking sound of horns at *The End.*

A pocket of silence, surrounded by riot, traveled down the aisle. I turned to see what was passing. Hector turned. It was Cookie. She fingered the Crucifix at her throat, pinkie running over the body of Jesus, arms outstretched, pulsing on her throat. My face turned among the ranks of profiles, staring, mouth wide open. Cookie looked, laughed, and said, "Whatcha doin', catchin' flies?" My ears burned, I closed my mouth and thought of Lon Chaney Jr. staring at the hair growing on his knuckles. "Ay what a barbarity," Hector said, as he perused Cookie's spectacular anatomy in the tight skirt and sweater. Hector's scream wailed through delight, horror, the permutations of all sexes. "*Ay Mami!* What a barbarity, a woman making such a show of what God gave her."

Popeye quaffed a can of spinach. Buck Rogers traveled to a star. The sound system sounded waterlogged. Buck Rogers' voice gurgled. The dark shot through with beams of light, bright blue threads of spring funneled through the holes in the roof, illuminated flocks of galoshes and caps, flying about; and cheers, pandemonium, gangs of boys limping Wolf Man-like into the aisle. Wizards of peripheral vision, they lurked in the vicinity of Cookie. On the screen, a soldier of the French Foreign Legion staggered, alone, under the blazing sun. Love had sent him into the desert. The roof of The Dump was porous as a sieve, all weather blew through the dark. I could smell spring and one unremitting wind of winter. Great thunder from outside. On the screen the legionnaire staggered across the technicolor desert, crying, "Water, water." The rain came through the roof, my head soaked, I cried, "Water, water." The legionnaire crawling across the desert cried, "Water," with everyone in the house taking up the cry, "Water, water," and the flood fell through the roof.

ABE AND IZZY

My soul ladles out sleep. The snoring I hear is not me, it is my wife, and I laugh because the sound is the only unbeautiful thing about her, and I would share the joke with my father but it is happening in a future that doesn't yet exist. My old man loosens the arm clamped around my neck, and with the other he gestures toward the crowd and explains, "I wanna buy him a pair of shoes." Someone is yelling, "Call the cops." Pop has me in a headlock, bent over at the waist I stare at the pavement. If I stretch my neck I can breathe and see the crowd that has gathered. I'm a veteran, in uniform, twenty-years old, and my father is strangling me. I struggle. My arms are around his waist. I attempt a bear hug, bending him backward to break his grip, but the old man is still too strong for me.

So there we are, in front of the shoe store, locked together, Abe and Izzy, like a hunk of erotic Hindu sculpture. His free hand clamps his chest, trembles, as though to keep the wild dog of his heart from jumping out of his ribs and running loose in the streets. He yells, "Why should he deny me? I'm his father, no?" The frowning woman with the headless pullet sticking out of her shopping bag nods and says, "Ingrates, every one of them." From somewhere at the center of the crowd an old woman's voice quavers, "My Arnold is a prince." "Look," Pop says, searching the crowd for the voice that said "My Arnold is a Prince." "I'm asking so much? I want to buy him shoes." The little bald guy standing next to the woman with the shopping bag studies my face. "Mr.," he says, "the boy is turning colors—now blue!" "Izzy, you alright?" Pop asks and loosens his hold. My ears are burning. I straighten up, rub my neck, and view the avenue. There are many stores. I want to go to the shops and shed my uniform, peel khaki for civilian garb. I have a pocket full of money. Pop surveys me, head to toe. "Please," he says, "let me buy you the shoes, nice, sporty two-toned." His hand gestures to the window full of shining shoes, "Florsheim," he says. "Listen," I say, returning us to the argument just before we got to the shoe store, "Roosevelt carried out Socialism on a stretcher." "Oh yeah," he says, "I know what's eatin' you, and you're just changin' the subject, Stalin was right to knock off Trotsky, see? That Leon was a pain in the ass intellectual." So just as I was about to say in the kitchen, before Korea, when Momma interrupted to hug and say good-bye and the dialectics had reached the point where it would wreck the furniture, I remind the old man that he had been a sucker for Roosevelt. "Sucker," I say. "Whatta you mean?" says Pop, his eyes gone glassy wet, face red. I jab the naked place. "Franklin Delano Roosevelt," I spit out, naming my old man's bimbo. "Oh yeah?" he says, "Oh yeah?" slipping his hand inside his shirt, fingering the laces of his truss. "Yeah," I say, "what did Roosevelt do for working people, but throw them a few crumbs? He saved his own kind, the millionaires." "What you know about it, Sonny Boy?" "I know that the world still belongs to the people who make money from money, or maybe you got a depreciation allowance for your back?" "Listen to him," Pop says, "your mother's womb was your soup kitchen, Sonny. You got rosy and chubby floatin' around in there; she went down to eighty pounds, she was all tits and eyes." So now he's gonna beat me over the head with that. Momma's flesh and blood, my bread and wine, "Whatta you want me to do? Living things are expensive." "So yeah," he says, smiling, "so let me at least get you the shoes."

Up and down the avenue shoppers move from store to store; some stop at the spectacle of us and join in the argument. I can hear from the loaded windows stacked to the sky, and all the voices of the jammed avenue a bawling, peripatetic harangue. Parents and children, wives and husbands, grandparents, everyone accusing and screaming. Car horns blare and honk. A small pickup truck goes by filling the air with the smell of herring. The letters on the side of the truck read, "Barney Greengrass the Sturgeon King." A merchant is cranking an iron handle, rolling up an awning that shades a window display. The store sells umbrellas, handbags, various accessories and lightweight folding chairs. I want to buy my mother one of the folding chairs. Momma loves the sun, illicitly. On occasion, on a bright warm day she allows herself a moment of standing by the kitchen window; thinking, no doubt, that the manmade world is a place unfit for children. I dream of the grave Jewish Madonna, indulging herself, seated in the folding chair in front of her building, basking in the sun. And I must find a suitable gift for my brother. There is a luggage store where I can buy a suitcase to replace my duffel bag, stuffed with underwear and books, which I've stored in a locker at Port Authority.

Pop is heating up again, and I know he'd mangle me, right here, if it weren't for his sense of the larger betrayal, the injustice at the heart of all. The labor theory of value does not apply to love. The most costly things cannot be earned. "So," he says, "you still doin' that writin'?" "I'm trying to learn." "Tryin' to learn? You gonna spend your life bein' a nudder unborn genius?" "I'm here," I insist. "For cryin' out loud, be a mensch. You got a mouth, you got words, fine, you could be a labor lawyer, do something real for people." A breeze makes Pops receding white hair stand on end. I say, "What about Steinbeck?" "What about him?" "He wrote *The Grapes of Wrath* and Congress passed laws to help the migrant workers." "All right," Pop says, "You just proved my point, you can open a mouth." "And Zola," I say, "he wasn't an enemy either, think what he did for Dreyfus." My father looks weary. "Okay wise guy, while you're scribblin', how you goin' to eat? What are you gonna do for a livin'?" "I'm thinking of maybe going back to school, becoming a teacher." "A teacher," he sighs, "okay, you're too nervous to steal." "Momma is waiting," I remind him, "and I have to get out of my soldier suit. She'll be happier to see me in civilian clothes." He says, "All right. But don't be an anti-Semite" which he pronounces "antuh-suh-mit," his accusation a warning that I'm in danger of the ultimate misanthropy—an antuh-suh-mit. "At least let me get you the shoes. Wait here, I know your size."

Pop rushes into Florsheim's. His broad back fills the doorway. I take off. I'm running. I've got a good lead on him, at least a block. I speed by people who look disapprovingly at me. I hear them shouting encouragement in my father's direction. I know they're pointing at my back as I turn the corner. I look over my shoulder and he is nowhere in sight. I look again, and there he is. He's coming on, he won't quit the chase. Tucked under his arm, like a football, is the box of shoes. I think I can outrun him.

In the Park

"Herbie is a little slow," his mother, Sophie Mintz hollered, "and nobody should take advantage." And in case anyone should forget, as she tended to as the day wore on, she'd thrust her head from the fourth story window, and yell, "Herbie, Herbie." When he didn't respond, she shrieked, "Swifty, Swifty!"

No one could remember who named twelve-year-old Herbert "Swifty." None of the street's wits claimed credit. The nicknaming, a baptism, during which his head was doused with cream soda, flooded recall and Swifty had difficulty remembering that his name had been Herbert. This was a time when truth couldn't be veiled by euphemism, and on the same street lived Frankie-One-Eye, Sammy the Gimp, Moshe the Gonif, and Vinnie Pazzo.

Swifty's father, Sol, wasn't so much taciturn as overwhelmed by the one great truth of his life; to all questions he answered, "I make a living." The statement had sufficed for a marriage proposal, and if there were greetings or inquiries that required mouthing something more, he never noticed; but, when confronted with a question regarding a plumbing problem, his trade, he would describe in vivid detail, clogged pipes, and sewage flow, recreating, when words failed, the sound of unimpeded water, the flushing of a toilet.

Old Man Levine, weathered into the stone stoop, rested his head on his arthritic fist grasping the handle of his cane, and said to Sophie Mintz on various occasions, "Not to worry Sophie, Swifty lives in God's time." Swifty, lingering under the blows of astonishment, eyes and mouth agape, stared at the luminescent marble in the palm of his hand. The boy he was playing with crouched at the curb, one knee on the pavement, the other lowered on the asphalt, his shadow straddling the pavement and the gutter. He squinted, forefinger and thumb cocked, aimed, and shot his marble, a red jumbo. He looked up and called, "Swifty, yo, Swifty." Swifty studied the marble in the palm of his hand. He heard faintly, "Swifty, yo Swifty," as his vision gathered in a mother further down the street squatting at the edge of the pavement and holding between her knees, a baby girl above the curb, the child's dress gathered up, panties around her ankles, the palms of the mother's hands cradled the undersides of the kid's thighs; the little girl's legs, from the knees down, dangled; her bare bottom hovered over the curb and she peed. The vision of the golden rivulet trickling down obscured Petey's claim on Swifty's attention.

Regarding stick-ball, Swifty could hit when he remembered to swing. One day he connected with what looked like a two-sewer home run; the ball flew high and arched, floating between roof tops and Swifty stood watching the ball chase a cloud. The other boys were shouting for him to run the bases. He stood and watched. A teammate shoved him. He stumbled, regained his footing and examined the sky. His teammates yelled. He heard a voice he was susceptible to, loped suddenly, and was nearly hit by a car. The vehicle veered toward the opposite curb and screeched to a stop. Swifty hardly noticed, never rounding third he continued to trot straight down the middle of the street and followed the cloud that had swallowed the ball until he and the cloud disappeared in the vicinity of the docks. When his mother remembered him, and cried, "Herbie-oy-Swifty," from the window, and there was no reply, neighbors pointed in the direction where Swifty had run until he was an illusion dwindling into the haze near the East River. Sophie charged down four flights of stairs screaming out of the building and searched for her son. Swifty perambulated in a mystery. Sophie and Swifty's circuits traversed, although they never met. Later at night, they encountered one another in the apartment. Sophie wept with relief, Swifty wept in sympathy.

On a Saturday late in the autumn the scent of snow could be detected among the smells of the shoe polish factory, the sugar factory, and the beer brewery. A group of boys had gathered to choose sides for a game of punch ball. Swifty wouldn't be chosen to play on either team. He stood, unperturbed, staring at Cosmo Leznick. Cosmo, studying the dregs, twisted his mouth in distaste: any selection foreordained defeat. Cosmo pointed to a boy staring at his feet, standing next to Swifty. Swifty, mouth agape, in what may have been taken for a smile, stood, his vision riveted on Cosmo. During the choosing of sides Cosmo had been scratching his crotch. He interpreted Swifty's smile as presumption, unspoken, but plain enough, and Cosmo wouldn't endure the insult alluding to his family's hygiene. He stopped scratching and popped Swifty. Swifty blinked and continued to stare. His nose throbbed and he stuck his tongue out to taste the blood. Sophie happened to be at the window. She appeared in the street. Cosmo had been about to lay down a flattened garbage can lid to serve as first base. She grabbed two fistfuls of his hair and yanked his head east and west, north and south. From the stoop Mr. Levine leaning forward on his cane, called to her in Yiddish saying she was creating a disgrace for the eyes of the gentiles. She ran back upstairs, locked herself in the apartment, and didn't appear at the window for the rest of the day. Cosmo's mother stood outside the locked door and spewed curses in Polish on the Mintz family. From that time on whenever Mrs. Leznick passed the Mintz family's door she paused to curse them; however, as she knew they were already an accursed people, she also entreated Jesus to remember his responsibility and punish them.

Buzzy Demarco, a countervailing spirit to Cosmo Leznick, was often the captain of the opposing team: stoop ball, stick ball, punch ball, and all the variants of baseball. Buzzy's authority derived from a supernatural grace. A pink Spaulding bouncing off the roof of a moving car, gaining altitude would appear to halt in midair and wait as Buzzy's flight described the symmetry of larger winged birds, and obedient gravity brought the ball to his hand.

There was also the ritual of Buzzy's summertime beneficence. Buzzy's friends, admirers, and the envious would seat themselves on the steps of the stoop to watch. Old Man Levine mounted there, grimaced, watched the feral children and thought that surely the coming of the Messiah couldn't be far off. As Tony's ice truck slowed for a delivery, Buzzy trotting a car-length behind the truck, accelerated, and within three strides leaped onto the flat bed of the truck, and slid a cake of ice off the tailgate, which exploded shards all over the gutter. Tony slammed on the brakes and shot out of the cab of the truck brandishing the ice tongs he swore would someday impale Buzzy's head. Buzzy was nowhere in sight. The ice man, who had once made an unwelcome advance toward Buzzy's widowed mother, retrieved the largest piece of ice from the street and swore revenge against Buzzy, a maiming worse than death, and touched his crotch in analogous genuflection. Everyone knew Tony meant it, and Buzzy, a fugitive most often in plain sight, took this danger as just one more responsibility. When Tony and his truck were gone kids bounded from the stoop steps, grabbed the gleaming wet chunks from the black hot asphalt, and sucked the cold diamonds.

Swifty was among Buzzy's worshipers. Although Swifty couldn't speculate whether fourteen-year-old Buzzy, honing his extraordinary talent, would two years hence box in the Golden Gloves. Buzzy would reappear in the street as the kids bent to harvest the ice from the gutter. Swifty, always a little too late, never would have snatched a piece if it weren't for Buzzy, who handed Swifty the melting gem. Swifty licked it. His eyes fixed on the slits of Buzzy's eyes, shaped like smiles, the dark light of his irises shining in his umber tinted face. Swifty gaped, suckled by ice.

On a Sunday, church bells ringing, Buzzy, pinnacled on a scrap of floor jutting out of the side of a tenement recently destroyed by fire, called to his followers climbing through the charred ruin. The half-dozen boys had progressed up above the fourth story and clung to the ladder and fire escapes attached to what had been the front of the building. Buzzy hadn't given Swifty permission to join in. He shook his head and said, "No, Swifty, stay here, on the block," and pointed to a group of younger children gathered in front of Swifty's building. Still, Swifty tagged along, ambling a distance behind the group led by Buzzy. The game was "Follow the Leader" and it was up to Buzzy to determine the level of risk all would try to meet. Swifty followed the gang at a half-block interval.

Three stories above the rubble piled in the street, Swifty opened a door to a chasm. The remains of the stairway that had shuddered under his weight trembled behind him, gaping space on either side of the steps. Suspended there, Swifty stretched his neck and looked below. Acrid wisps of smoke made his eyes tear. Looking down he saw the tenement's coal bin, like a jewel box, glowing. Others were calling from the ladder and fire escapes attached to one of the tenement's two remaining roofless walls. The wind moving the clouds surrounding the five story high wall made it appear to sway; the smashed windows dribbled ribbons of smoke. Vapors of mortar dust drifting from between the bricks blew in the air. The wall, and the fire escapes and ladder attached to it, seemed to list in the wind.

Swifty heard them calling his name. He saw Buzzy riding the scrap of floor among the clouds, exhorting the boys below, frozen to the ladder and fire escapes. Buzzy hollered for them to continue the climb. A fragment of a vestibule made a narrow bridge between the two walls. A kitchen at the further end of the bridge rested on what looked like the outcropping of a giant, concrete mushroom, spawned from the blackened brick walls. The kitchen, with the four chairs and table, was inhabited by pigeons strutting and pecking on the table. At the outermost lip of the kitchen floor one could view the East River and the Manhattan skyline; and hanging from below the concrete outcropping an entanglement of wire mesh, a network of girders and pipes the boys could climb down leaving a twelve-foot drop to the sidewalk. But to reach the bridge the boys would have to continue their climb up the ladder and fire escapes to join Buzzy on the floating scrap of floor and then, one at a time, leap into the air.

Swifty stood in the doorway of sky. He was aloft as Buzzy was aloft, saying his name. Swifty couldn't remember how he got there, but he was comfortable as he was in the playground, standing on a swing, grasping the narrow links of chain on either side, bending his knees and pumping himself higher and higher into the sky. Now he bent his knees and rested the palms of his hands on the doorframe, navigating his flight. Buzzy was yelling, "Bennie, Joey, keep goin.'" Swifty felt wind whoosh by his ears, the sound like Mama's lips at his ear pleading, "Give me loving." He'd reach his arms around her, far as they would go, hug her hips, his face sinking into the great cushion of her belly. "Give me loving," she wept. He'd maneuver his head so that he could breathe and repeat "loving," the tip of his tongue touching the roof of his mouth. Poppa only said, "Nah!" heaping food on his plate, and "Nah!" handing him a slice of bread. Sometimes Mama screamed, "Give me loving." Then Swifty was scared.

The prism of Swifty's seeing framed Louie falling from the ladder; the fathom of sky that framed him empty in the instant his cry dissipated. Louie would never walk again. People blamed Buzzy. The boys who had climbed the ruin of the burned building said that the fault wasn't really Buzzy's. They said everyone had become distracted by Swifty in the doorway of sky; he had caused the accident. Swifty knew the word "accident." It felt like his mother's breath brushing his ear, when she pleaded, "Give me loving." Within weeks the boys' assertion that it was Swifty who had caused Louie to wind up in a wheelchair became the prevailing belief. Everyone said that Swifty had hexed Louie, not deliberately; but he was a jinx, susceptible to the malocchio, the tumult of cacodemons at play in the shadow of his dumb wonder. The gossip reached Sophie. She would have argued against it but her waxing unhappiness convinced her of the futility of opposing such talk. However, she did take the precaution of dropping a pinch of salt in Swifty's pants pocket to weaken the force of blaming.

Sophie under siege behind her locked door heard Mrs. Leznick curse, "*Paskuddniak!*" But Sophie knew her apartment was immaculate. She scrubbed the floors on her hands and knees. Stood on a ladder and washed the walls. The odor of disinfectant was the perfume of her home. The accusation and curse "Filth" that Mrs. Leznick spat at her door was ameliorated by Sophie's scouring and knowledge of Sol's labor that kept faucets running and toilets flushing.

Sophie cried and confessed to the simmering pot roast that she couldn't remember Swifty every minute of the day. She considered tying him to his bed but decided that was too cruel.

As Swifty approached a group of boys, they faded and reappeared at a greater distance. Mothers pulled their children away when Swifty came near, and the distance between Swifty and other children remained constant. He saw the mothers' faces whispering, and knew it was about him. Only Old Man Levine mounted on the stoop made coaxing sounds. And it began to snow.

The bus was moving slowly through the slush, the chains on the tires ringing. Swifty thought he saw Buzzy. The runner outpaced the cloud of gas he was striding in and leaped onto the back of the bus. His feet resting on the rear bumper, he clung to the rim of the bus's oblong rear window, and bent his knees, riding the undulations, letting every bounce shape his posture. Voices from the stoop called out in scofflaw affirmation, "Hitchin' on the wagon, hitchin' on the wagon." And Swifty was off, chasing the bus as it slowed to a stop.

The wheels clanged. Swifty rode, clinging to the back of the bus, his legs flexing and thrusting like a swimmer riding the swell of a wave. From inside the bus a kid pressed his face against the rear window. The boy's nose flattened against the glass into a pig's snout; he rolled his eyes. The boy's cheeks ballooned and his eyes squeezed shut. The face gnashed teeth. Swifty looked away, up at the gray sky shedding snow. A surf of clouds raced along with the bus, invisibly tethered to Swifty's vision. The rooftops sped along, and a flock of pigeons rolled out of sight carried by the wind. And thick, wet snowflakes fell.

The boy clinging to the back of the bus wasn't Buzzy, and he jumped off after two blocks. Swifty tightened his grip on the metal rim that bordered the rear window. Gas fumes wafted around his head. The breeze buffed his cheeks. He thrust his head out of the cloud of gas and gulped air. A quivering radiated up his spine, humming the ride in his bones.

The knocking inside the rear window was urgent. The boy unpressed his face from the window, shouting warning, rapping on the glass. An old woman seated next to the boy scowled. Swifty knew what to do. The wheels hissed. The bus rocked to a stop.

He was halfway down the street when the bus driver gave up the chase several paces beyond the rear bumper, as was always the case; the driver stood, shouted warning and returned to the inside of the bus.

Swifty strolled along a street of neat brownstone buildings. Everything had turned white. He smelled something delicious. Under the rolled-up awning the store front window of Ernie's Rib Joint was open. The savory breeze pulled a stream of brown men through the doorway. Swifty stood for a while in the mouth-watering aroma, and then wandered on. His hands hurt with the cold, he crossed his arms over his chest and sheltered his hands under his armpits.

"Hey snowflake, stop where you at." The three boys came up to him. Two were smiling. The one who wasn't smiling stood close to Swifty and said, "You woofin' at me?" Swifty looked at the two boys who couldn't stop laughing. The angry one grabbed the front of Swifty's jacket and said, "I ain't jokin', what you doin' paradin' your dumb ass on my street? Where you from, little ofay?" Swifty recited his address. The two laughing boys convulsed into a dance around Swifty. The angry one shouted, "I'm serious," and cuffed Swifty's ear. "Lemme see," the angry one said, "what's in your pockets." The two who had been laughing became attentive. Swifty turned his pants pockets inside out. From one pocket salt drifted down. Swifty raised the hand that had pulled out the pocket and tasted the tips of his fingers. The boys howled, "Nasty!" The angry one pantomimed a punch he didn't throw.

A stout brown woman carrying a shopping bag stepped between Swifty and the boys. "What you up to here?" The angry one said, nodding toward Swifty, "He lookin' for trouble." One of the laughing boys said, "Sheeet, anyone can see he a born fool." The woman rested the clinking, shopping bag full of empty bottles on the sidewalk, and said, "Boy, when you talk around me you better mind your language." The boy said "Sheeet" again. "Smell that," the woman said, and put her fist under his nose. The boy took a step back. "I was jus' sayin' anyone can see he dumb by nature." The woman studied Swifty's face. "Child," she said, "you can close your mouth." Swifty did. "And wipe your nose." Swifty raised his sleeve to his nose, and the woman said, "Wait." She opened her purse, removed a tissue and handed it to Swifty. She guided his hand with the tissue to his nose. "That's right," she said. "Now," she said, looking away from Swifty, standing there with his jacket and pants pockets turned out, "was you all gonna rob this child?" "We jus' playin' with him," the two who'd been laughing said. The angry one said, "Maybe he jus' some kind a runty nut, but he best keep to his home block anyways. He don't belong here." The woman took a closer look at Swifty as he appeared completely absorbed watching her. "Listen," she said, "whether he be a little simple or just carried away appreciatin' ain't no cause for robbery. Now you boys be on your way, and stay out a mischief, you hear?"

The stout brown lady told Swifty to stuff his pockets in and loaded three empty milk bottles in his arms. She pointed to a grocery store. "Now, you give the grocery man these here empties, and he give you six cent, a nickel to ride, and a penny for what you want. You know your way home, child?" Swifty recited his address. The lady said, "Go now," Swifty lingered, wanting to stay in the warm eddies of the woman's voice. She smiled and pointed at the grocery. They stood looking at one another. She started to walk away and Swifty followed her. She stopped, turned and said, "Go on now" pointing once more at the grocery.

Seated in the bus Swifty watched the snow-covered streets roll by. The rushing sky and rooftops lashed to his scrutiny by the thinnest membranes of light; again, he recited his address. A man seated across from him raised his head from a newspaper, looked at Swifty and ducked back behind the newspaper. The bus turned and went down a steep street.

Looking through his breath on the window he saw the faint reflection of the boy that was him, the falling snow, and two boys fencing with large, frozen fish. Passengers on the bus shouted, "Look." Boys all over the street threw fish at one another and whacked each other over the head and shoulders with fish. The bus maneuvered through the narrow street slowly. Fish were strewn all over the gutter; heads and tails, and glittering ice. A spiral of fish scales swirled, shining among the snow drops. A man seated in the back of the bus began to shout angrily in a language Swifty had never heard. Someone yelled back in English, "Believe me, the little bastards ain't orphans. It's the parents they should put in jail!" The bus driver said, "Amen to that." Snowballs thudded against the windows and sides of the slow-moving bus. A woman passenger screamed and ducked her head toward her lap as a snowball splattered against the window where she was seated. Nuggets of ice and fish heads bounced off the bus. Swifty saw the boys take aim. Gleaming, somersaulting through air the fish guts flew like something alive, and smacked the window where Swifty stared. His head recoiled as though he'd been punched. The entrails slithered down the window. One round, stumpy babushka adjusted her kerchief, tightened the knot under her chin, and with a paper shopping bag hanging from her hand tottered to the rear door. "Stop," she wailed. The bus rocked to a halt. She swayed. The doors whooshed open. "Leo!" she cried, "Leo!" The bus driver yelled, "Give it to him good! Warm his pants." A fish head landed on the floor near the babushka's feet. She howled, "Leo, don't come home or you'll make me a murderer." All the passengers, except for the man reading the newspaper were yelling. The babushka stepped down and moved toward the melee. At the opposite curb there was a truck parked halfway up on the sidewalk, tilted to the driver's side, the right rear tire pancaked. Two boys stood on the tailgate and emptied bushel baskets of fish and crushed ice into the gutter. Swifty looked for Buzzy. Fish thumped off the side of the bus. The driver maneuvered the bus around the truck and the kids pounding each other with fish. At the corner the bus turned and picked up speed. Swifty reached up and pulled the cord. The bus didn't stop. He stood up, held onto a pole with one hand and with the other pulled the cord again. The bus sped on. Swifty looked toward the bus driver, he couldn't think of what to say. He saw unfamiliar streets flying by. At last the bus stopped. The rear doors opened. Swifty stepped down, off the bus.

The air was dense with snow. The corridor of trees, white. Next to a boarded-up snow-domed kiosk was an entrance to a park. The paths and the benches were empty and white. Swifty had never heard such quiet. Except for his chilled feet he wasn't very cold. He tasted his salty fingertip, stuck his tongue out and lapped in the moisture. He looked behind him and saw the long trail of his footprints disappearing near the hedges where he'd entered the park. He walked in the quiet, following his shadow and exhaled little clouds of breath. The path turned, Swifty turned with it. Through the white flecked silence he heard wheezing. The sound grew louder. He came closer. He passed the breathing body heaped on the bench under a rug. The face had the pink sheen of a lollipop wrapped in cellophane. The lips trembled. The man's arms hung down, his fingertips sunk in the snow. Under the bench a brown bottle with a picture of three roses on it peaked a hillock of slush. The snow made all of the man white, except for his glistening pink face. Between the upright slabs of his shoes and the ragged cuffs of his pants, coils of newspaper squeezed out over his milky blue ankles. Swifty walked faster. The man's puling wheeze followed him. Swifty ran until he could no longer hear it.

Footprints in what had been the smooth expanse of snow appeared; he stopped, lifted his leg and placed his foot into the recess and his foot fit exactly. On either side of him the white sloping grounds swelled, untouched. His feet inside his sodden shoes were damp and chilled. He walked in slow motion placing his feet in the indentations as if he'd made these footprints earlier, and now he was playing follow-the-leader, carrying himself somewhere he'd started trudging to long ago. Gingerly he lowered each foot into each footprint, following the trail laid out in front of him. After a while he strode less carefully, exploding the footprints into white dust, but kept to the path that led him toward the sound of barking.

The seal was perched at the top of a stone pyramid, head lifted, barking. There was no one else at the iron railing that encircled the pool of water. A breathing hump rose from the surface of water, floated for an instant and sunk. The seal on top of the pyramid leaped, gliding in the air; it rode the arc it shaped down into the water, splashed and vanished. Swifty studied the water. The seal didn't reappear.

Beyond the pool and the cage with the largest black cat Swifty had ever seen was a towering cage with a giant tree inside it. Swifty studied the caged, birdless tree, walked on and thought he saw, not too far away, a uniformed park attendant disappear into a great stone house, from which came the sound of creatures he couldn't imagine.

It was getting near to dusk. He was shivering. Three boys walking toward him waved. He stood still, waiting for them to disappear, but they came nearer, gesturing for him to join them. As they turned into another path they called to him, whistling. Heavy-footed in the snow, he trotted after them.

The tall one wore a leather aviator's cap, goggles, and was wrapped in a tent-like military coat, festooned with flaps, buckles, and brass buttons. The littlest one, in a red sweater, shivered. His eyes were watery, and he gnawed at his raw fist. The third was short, round, every part of him seemed swollen; he wore a flannel shirt, unbuttoned, corduroy pants, and sneakers. On top of his head, a baseball cap with the visor turned behind his head; he was sweating and smoking the stub of a cigarette. The tall one raised the goggles and placed them on his leather encased forehead. "You got a cigarette?" Swifty shrugged. The fat one said, "This little pisser got nothin'," The tall one said, "It's snowy Saturday and we own the joint, but don't worry we ain't gonna hurt you. You come to see the hellephants? Big sons of bitches ain't they?" Swifty looked beyond the railing down the deep stone incline that led to a trench filled with water; beyond it, a cobble stone hill climbed to a plateau, where two elephants raised straw in their curling trunks to their mouths. Behind the elephants stood their immense house. Swifty had never seen any living thing so large, so imperturbable. The enormous fans of their ears moved slowly. Steam rose from their haunches. "Lissen," the tall boy said, "You're gonna trade your jacket for my brudder's sweater. Okay gimmee." Swifty watched the elephants. Monumental, they moved ever so slightly, like motion in the fluid tempo of a dream. The tall boy unbuttoned Swifty's jacket. Swifty turned obligingly. He pulled his arms out of the sleeves. For a moment he couldn't see anything as the sweater that the little guy had been wearing was pulled over his head. But then he saw the elephants again, the legs like tree trunks, enormity moving.

The snowball looped out of the sky. The littlest one, wearing Swifty's jacket, took his bloodied knuckle from his mouth and pitched a snowball, high. The three were throwing. The snowballs curved in the sky, splashed into the trench of water, and plopped near the elephants, tranquilly eating. Swifty turned from the immense quiet of the elephants to the murderous faces of the boys: such concentrated vehemence in their intention, rehearsing slaughter they bellowed "Fuck! Bastard! Bitch!" and Swifty cried. As if the size and imperturbability of the beasts had offended them, the boys let go barrage after barrage and cursed. Swifty turned his head from the boys to the elephants, back to the boys; frantic, dizzy, his eyes retained the image of their ferocity; the turning of his head blurred the sight of the huge indifferent animals with the splotches of snowballs melting down their sides. Swifty at the center of the boys' war dance, they howled "Fuck! Bastard! Bitch!" Swifty's weeping wracked his body.

The tall one in the aviator's cap and goggles hollered "Cease fire!" The boys froze in place, grinning. "Look at that," the one in the goggles said to Swifty, "Look at that," he commanded, pointing to a purple Jelly Baby under the iron railing, sheltered from the snow. Next to the purple one was a yellow one, the size of a nickel. Slowly Swifty's tremors ebbed and he watched the boy peel the candy from the ground, kiss it, hold it up to the sky, and say, just before he put it in his mouth, "Kiss it up to God. He pointed to the yellow Jelly Baby and directed Swifty to do the same. Swifty held it in his hand. "Go on, go on. Kiss it up to God." Swifty kissed it and raised his hand with the candy above his head. "Yeah, awright, you can eat it now." Swifty put it in his mouth. It was sweet. "See you around," the boys said and marched away, while Swifty searched under the rail for more candy he could kiss up to God and eat.

The dark warmed him. When he looked up through the haze of falling snow he saw the white ball of the moon extricating itself from the tree's branches. Home was far away, and anyway he didn't want to go there. He walked deeper into the park, wading in the white dunes that had swallowed the streets and buildings, the billowing white going on and on until it was everything.

FAR EAST

In the heat, outside the Mess Hall, the flies buzzing around my head, I'd almost become acclimated to my own stink as I separated edible from inedible garbage. Master Sergeant Crawford checked periodically to make sure that I plunged my arm deep enough into the garbage can to retrieve from the rancid creamed chipped beef, rinds, bones, and rotting fruit, any cigarette butts and cardboard containers that the troopers had dumped and scraped from their food trays as they filed out of the Mess Hall. I was responsible for removing anything that could interfere with the digestion of pigs, as the military sold and or contributed the swill to farmers, and the pigs, it was said, thrived on army slop.

I washed and scoured the garbage cans until they gleamed. Before separating edible from inedible garbage, I washed pots and pans in the Mess Hall. I cleaned the Mess Hall grease trap. I dug a trench where Sergeant Crawford entombed a cigarette butt. A late sunny afternoon found me on the simmering metal roof of the Mess Hall filing away rust spots.

On the roof, a haze before my eyes, drops of sweat hung from my nose and fell on my lips. My left shoulder ached.

Two MPs had found me in an alley near a sailor, crapped out and feeling no pain. The MPs nudged me, yanked me upright, dragging me until my feet found the pavement. I was in uniform. Disheveled, shoelaces untied, my pants torn at the knee, but in uniform.

Captain Roscoe, company commander at the base in Tokyo where I took company punishment and waited for a decision regarding my possible court martial, looked me up and down and drawled, "I didn't know they could stack shit that high. Still, you're one lucky bastard. If you had been found out of uniform the charge would not be AWOL but desertion and then your sorry ass would be lookin' at thirty years. Did your poor mama have any children that lived?"

Each morning, I stood at attention in my fatigues at the center of the quad, alone except for Sergeant Crawford. He bellowed "cruit," short for recruit. "Your soul may belong to Jesus, but your ass belongs to me." Cooking on the Mess Hall roof under hot heaven on a day I feared would never end, I was tempted to barter with the ultimate. The enticement frightened me. It could be a symptom of corruption. Teeth clenched, I argued the thought is not the deed. I'd considered making a promise a vow in exchange for a punishment, more lenient than toiling in garbage forever. A short time after reveille, groggy, I asked Sergeant Crawford to please repeat what he said. I had difficulty believing what I'd heard. The day I feared would never end had arrived. I recalled the respite of shade followed by the disquiet of my conscience instigated. Not sure that the vague recollection of scuffling was part of R and R or some other occasion, Sergeant Crawford conveyed the news. He itemized my good luck as a cautionary tale. He noted that I was a natural-born fuck-up. Sergeant Crawford's hand went to his crotch, he lifted his testicles, the reverent touching of his escutcheon emblem of virility and defiance.

Sergeant Crawford went on to say I would not be court-martialed but shipped to Korea where, the brass believed the armistice would never hold, and my otherwise useless ass would be put in harm's way in the service of my country. In the meantime, before the inevitable hostilities, I was busted, losing my one stripe. I'd take the corresponding pay cut, and before shipping me to Korea, where I'd been headed in the first place, before I violated my twenty-four-hour pass, the Army would be certain to change my MOS, that is my military occupational specialty. My MOS was no longer clerk typist, privileged duty; now I was a body and fender man and I'd work in the motor pool.

In the new foreign country no one shot at me. From time to time we were required to play war games. We marched, climbed up and down mountains under full packs, M1 rifles slung over our shoulders. We camped in tents on hard ground in the cold, the foulest weather chosen for these exercises, but the maneuvers felt like the price of entitlement. For the most part it was an odd, cushy life. Every GI suddenly, for the first and perhaps the only time in his life, was a rich man. The eagle shat at the end of each month and every soldier's pocket packed a fortune, the omnipotent American dollar, the richest coin in the world. Fate's survivors, living lavishly between the ordained slaughters, urban peasant or redneck, we were chosen for a privileged existence. Even those who had grown up hungry and shoeless, now had servants and complained of the difficulty of getting reliable help.

Koreans, grown men and boys, cleaned and prepared the barracks for inspection. They did the laundry, spit shined our boots, made up our bunks in the morning, and pulled KP duty. All this cost each GI a dollar a month. The Koreans who had such employment considered themselves fortunate: what they earned was sufficient to support a large family.

The casualties among the troops were primarily venereal. I remained faithful to something I couldn't name. There was a small but well-stocked library on the base. I taped to the inside of my wall locker door lists of new words and their definitions. Walking from the barracks or the Mess Hall to the Motor Pool, my life between reveille and taps settled into a routine. I'd look out into the bay. I had never seen anything like it before. When the tide was out the ocean disappeared. At the horizon, where the sky rested on the periphery of the earth, miles out, mud flats rich with alluvial manna puckered and breathed. When the Red Sea parted did the path resemble this? I learned that the laboring shrouds in the distance were women scavenging shellfish and other edibles from the exposed ocean floor. The work had to be done before the tide came in.

In the Motor Pool, an immense Quonset hut, jeeps and trucks were serviced. Three Korean men and I worked with a squad of GI mechanics, primarily to fetch and carry. The throbbing engines, clanging of metal on metal, and shouting human voices echoed as in a cave. The racket augmented with hand signs, portable radios blared rock and roll.

The men gathered around each truck as if it were a mastodon they cared for lovingly.

Most of the men revered Sergeant Russell. He was a combat veteran awarded many medals, which he would only wear under orders during obligatory military ceremonies. The creases in his khaki trousers were razor sharp, his brass belt buckle shined, the whole lean muscular form of the soldier starched and immaculate throughout the day in defiance of all weather. His face was a dream of American innocence, rugged, righteous, and clear-eyed.

I had confessed right off that in spite of my MOS I was not a body and fender man, didn't know anything about it, indeed, didn't have a driver's license; living in New York as a civilian I had availed myself of public transportation and hadn't found it necessary to learn how to drive. Sergeant Russell looked perplexed, then irritated, as if my calm were a form of impudence. I hesitated, wasn't sure how or if I should try to explain that I hadn't meant to appear insubordinate; but something blocked me from justifying myself, and then I thought that after all there was something in me that was insubordinate. Sergeant Russell studied me. I heard Corporal Bickford standing close by with a lit match in his hand, waiting to light the cigarette that dangled from Sergeant Russell's lip, mutter, "Jew York." This designation offered by the corporal to the sergeant was an explanation to demystify the ineffable.

When I agreed, without a sign of protest, to work along with the Koreans, fetching and hauling, Sergeant Russell looked troubled. He stared at me waiting for some response I failed to provide, and finally concluding that my acceptance was in some way subversive, he said that he would keep a close watch on me, and I'd better keep to my duties. I said, "Yes, sir." Sergeant Russell said, "Don't call me sir, I work for a fuckin' livin."

I had my evenings. I had the night and I was content. I was more than content, I was enchanted. I'd come across the work of William Faulkner at the post library and I spent the next year itinerant, wandering along through Joe Christmas's tragic misadventure in *Light in August*, *The Old Man* lost in the flood, followed Addy Bundren's coffin, also swept away by rampaging water in *As I Lay Dying*, as I traveled the stately, convoluted, brilliant rhetoric that sounded like God trying to unravel his secrets.

More than a month passed and I considered how the brutalization of the foundling Joe Christmas was the antithesis of the Nativity. Meanwhile along with Mr. Sung, Mr. Kim, and Mr. Shin, I hurried to fetch screw drivers, pliers, lug wrench, spanner wrench, learned to identify and carry the filler wrench for changing oil, the breaker bar to break rust and loosen nuts, alligator clips for the charger, pulled the floor jack and carried batteries across the booming length of the Motor Pool and learned that despite the look of mockery on PFC Glidding's red face, he hadn't actually called me a "creep." I was slow to take offense, slow to understand the resentment building in my own dark. I was as surprised as PFC Glidding when I grabbed him by the lapels of his fatigue jacket and slammed him against the side of the Jeep. Several guys jumped in and separated us.

Standing before Sergeant Russell I expected that he was about to read me the riot act and that this time I was in deep shit. Sergeant Russell pointed at the floor and commanded, "Look at that!" "What?" "That, Kominsky! Open your damn eyes!" I looked at a low platform with four wheels, very close to the floor that I recognized as a device for a mechanic to lay on as he slid himself below the belly of a vehicle. "That," barked Sergeant Russell, "is called a creeper." Sergeant Russell almost smiled. Slowly it dawned on me: Sergeant Russell had been waiting for a reassuring sign from me. My ready acceptance to work with Koreans had struck Sergeant Russell as a symptom of some malfeasance or idiocy. The absence on my part of any detectable amour propre had alarmed the sergeant and confirmed his forebodings of the future of the human race.

However, Sergeant Russell mitigated my duties by also making me his orderly. This meant some respite from hauling tools and machine parts. I would deliver paperwork to the clerk typist at headquarters, purchase cigarettes for Sergeant Russell at the PX and bring coffee from the Mess Hall. Neither Sergeant Russell nor Corporal Bickford, who had offered to unravel the mystery of me by whispering in Sergeant Russell's ear "Jew York" ever engaged me in conversation. I felt that their tolerance was based on the premise that my proximity to them, and especially to Sergeant Russell, was salutary in itself. They conversed and I could overhear whatever it was I was attentive enough to retain and thus possibly improve myself.

I had reached a point where the weight of whatever I carried provided gratification. The sweat that ran down my back confirmed a sense of growing strength, and if I was demonstrably crazy, I wasn't so much out of my mind as deeper in it, a strange place.

One day after pulling and lifting a hand truck loaded with a tank of gas and an acetylene torch across the floor, littered with tools and tires, I returned to a grave-looking Sergeant Russell, sitting like a heartbroken monarch behind his desk. Corporal Bickford was bent to Sergeant Russell's ear. He appeared to be consoling him. I stood there for some time taking on sufficient presence to become visible. The rain banging on the vast metal roof was torrential and deafening. Wiping sweat out of my eyes I imagined heaven in a promethean frenzy vomiting every tool there ever was or would be, all of it thundering on the roof hastening the end of the known world. The work continued, men bellowed and exchanged hand signs. The portable radios blared country western music and rock and roll. As I became visible to Sergeant Russell and Corporal Bickford, I remembered that as I had made my way across the cluttered floor, weaving the loaded hand truck around obstacles and, when necessary, lifting it, I'd had a moment of panic. The tremendous noise bombed the place in my mind where I might abide and I stopped, lost, disoriented. It was then that I saw Mr. Kim. He was standing next to a mechanic near the open hood of a truck, pointing at some part of the engine. I stared at Mr. Kim. His eyes met my gaze for an instant. He seemed to emanate his own quiet.

I found myself studying Mr. Kim. He was aware that I was watching him. If he was affronted by my staring nothing in his face or body language revealed his displeasure. Mr. Kim concentrated on the task at hand. His face reflected neither ease nor effort. I considered my face, which could be read by nearly anyone. After a time, I saw that the fingers of his left hand, except for his thumb were gone, and despite what might seem a disability, he hauled heavy equipment. His small compact body, the rolled-up sleeves of his fatigue blouse, revealed the slim unmuscled arms of a boy.

I heard from one of the GIs and from the ingratiating Mr. Sung who lived in the same village as Mr. Kim, that during World War II, at the time of the Japanese occupation, Mr. Kim had assumed the blame for an act he didn't commit to spare a terrified relative, and a Japanese officer, in reprisal, raised his sword and lopped off the four fingers of Mr. Kim's left hand.

Corporal Bickford pressed his fingers to his shirt pockets. I didn't get it. Sergeant Russell sat in his chair looking stoic. Finally, I understood and bummed a couple of cigarettes for Sergeant Russell, and extended my hand for money so that I could go to the PX and buy a carton of cigarettes.

When I returned with the cigarettes, which I managed to keep dry by keeping my hands clamped around them deep in my trouser pockets, I stood looking like someone who had barely survived drowning. Sergeant Russell sent me out again into the downpour to deliver a report to the clerk-typist. When I returned from the clerk-typist the rain began to subside.

Nevertheless Mr. Kim's patient study of the entire vehicle while making the most of his six fingers and four stumps found the place where and why the vehicle failed. Mr. Kim's English was limited, still the articulation of his remaining fingers arms, legs made a graceful didactic pantomime. A few mechanics rehearsed Mr. Kim's illustrations. Some mechanic's intimate restoration of vehicles precluded alien instruction.

Sergeant Russell suspected that Mr. Kim's ability to detect what was wrong with an engine was the benign aspect of something diabolical. Tools were missing. "Stolen," Corporal Bickford said. Sergeant Russell and Corporal Bickford were certain that one or more of the Koreans were responsible for the theft. The other men commented on the legendary stealth and agility of the Korean thieves known as Slicky Boys. One of the men told the story of the lieutenant in Seoul who had been driving his jeep and had not come to a complete stop until he reached his destination; then he found that the spare tire that had been screwed on to the back of the jeep was gone.

Because of Mr. Kim's wizardry Sergeant Russell and Corporal Bickford questioned him first. They made plain that they believed that he knew which of his countrymen were guilty of the theft. Mr. Kim stood and listened. Corporal Bickford said it was possible that Mr. Kim was the leader of the thieves; the Slicky Boys were probably relatives. Mr. Kim stood, listening, studying their faces and at last said, "Not so." As the interrogation went on and Sergeant Russell waited for a reply from Mr. Kim, Mr. Kim said, "Hungry people sometime number ten." In the pidgin that the GIs and Koreans employed to understand one another, in all things that were "number ten" was the worst and what was "number one" the very best. As I watched the faces of Corporal Bickford, Mr. Kim, and Sergeant Russell, I saw a look of distaste curl the sergeant's lips as he stared at Mr. Kim. Sergeant Russell, as he later tried to explain to the corporal, had concluded that Mr. Kim was one who neither required forgiveness nor did he need to forgive. And this too, testified to Sergeant Russell's sense of the fallen world.

I lost sight of Mr. Kim. He must have been working in the north end of the garage. The concern with the theft of the tools, like the tools themselves, disappeared into a resentful acceptance, a kind of forgetfulness predicated on the expectation that someday the tools would appear again in the black market.

I was still searching for a glimpse of Mr. Kim during the morning that I rolled the worn Jeep tires to the storage shed and made a couple of coffee runs to the Mess Hall. Corporal Bickford was tending to Sergeant Russell's hangover. Sergeant Russell, as usual, appeared to be his immaculate, soldierly self, only the dark pockets under his eyes suggested that he was in rough shape. Corporal Bickford ministered to Sergeant Russell seated at his desk, the sergeant's head propped in his right hand, his elbow on the desk, a tableau I passed again and again as I delivered coffee, paperwork, cigarettes; Corporal Bickford was reminding Sergeant Russell to write to his wife. After a time Sergeant Russell said something about his distrust of the desire he felt for the Korean woman he was shacked up with in the village. Corporal Bickford counseled that we must take our pleasures where we find them and said something suggesting the wisdom of Sergeant Russell's economy, fiscal and emotional.

As the long day continued I heard fragments of a discussion between Sergeant Russell and Corporal Bickford concerning original sin. The two soldiers appeared to be offering one another pardons. Corporal Bickford reminded Sergeant Russell that man's tendency to depravity was the result of Adam's disobedience, and there wasn't a damned thing either of them could do to change that. "Hell's bells," said the sergeant, and he reminded the corporal that the mess had started when the original bitch, Eve, who couldn't stand prosperity, nagged Adam, "Take a bite of the apple, honey, take a bite."

Close to chow time Sergeant Russell spoke of the great love of his life, of how he'd been betrayed, and how nothing in his life could have prepared him for this.

As I came and went I heard Sergeant Russell speak of his twenty years of devotion. He testified to the corporal that he had given the best of himself to the relationship, and now he had nothing more to give.

Toward twilight, Corporal Bickford summoned me out of the void to get a book of matches so he could light the Sergeant's cigarette. I materialized where I had been, standing at ease by the side of the desk. Corporal Bickford said he couldn't argue with Sergeant Russel's conclusion. Sergeant Russell said again, "Hell's bells, twenty years!" I wondered whether Sergeant Russell's wife back in the states had been unfaithful to him; perhaps she'd sent him a "Dear John" letter, or maybe the allure of the Korean woman he was shacked up with was so powerful that in spite of the sergeant's misgivings now he had to acknowledge his estrangement from his wife and reinvent his life whatever the cost in grief and confusion. I felt sympathy for Mrs. Russell: being an Army wife is difficult, given the frequent and long separations. The sergeant had never mentioned children.

As I put the pieces together, coming and going, I gathered that Sergeant Russell, a child of the Depression, from Arkansas, had for the first time in his life been well shod when he went to court his first love, the wife I assumed he now contemplated divorcing. As Sergeant Russell spoke he revealed a special fondness for the word "behooves" as in "it would behoove you mens to study how things work in this man's army."

I had moved on to the *The Sound and the Fury* and as I tried to make sense of the world sounding in Benjy the Idiot's head—landscape, green, fence, hole in the ground, flag and Benjy's moaning—I saw the golf course and my attention wandered. I lifted my head from the book. It was early evening. There was only one other GI in the library and he was asleep in a large leather chair, snoring softly. The library would close in about an hour. It was still close enough to the most recent payday so that the barracks might be deserted and quiet and I could read there. My empathy for Benjy disturbed me. I felt drowsy and haunted by a childlike intuition that I was the avatar of some idiocy that I would never understand. I remembered that when Corporal Bickford looked at me, actually saw me, it was always with suspicion. I'd almost become accustomed to this and still there was something in me responding to the expectation that I ought to explain myself to the corporal if I could, but as the corporal's face conveyed that I was not only a mystery hardly worth the trouble, I was also a contagion of some kind, I veered between feelings of "fuck you" and the temptation to identify myself as a human citizen of some unknown worth.

What I assumed about the Corporal's life, what I'd heard and gathered from what he was not inclined to keep secret, when he spoke to Sergeant Russell and I stood close by awaiting my next order, was that in spite of seventeen years in the army the corporal had never been in combat. Corporal Bickford lowered his voice and said that he wanted to think of himself as a soldier and yet, he had doubts. Sergeant Russell assured Corporal Bickford that the shit was bound to hit the fan again; the Reds were certain to cross the 38th Parallel and the corporal could count on being in the thick of it. As far as the sergeant was concerned he'd be "long gone, retired." He had hoped, he repeated to the corporal, to be a thirty-year man, but the traitor from Missouri, whom he'd actually voted for, ruined it all. The corporal laughed and said that he hoped the sergeant didn't hold it against him that he came from Missouri. The sergeant smiled and reminded the corporal that the corporal's tending his sergeant's hangovers had prevented or at least curtailed the corporal's drinking, forestalling the trouble that would result in the corporal's being busted again; to say nothing of the booze that would darken Corporal Bickford's Injun red complexion so that no one would ever take him for a white man. They laughed. Sergeant Russell again cursed, "Harry the traitor."

I'd misunderstood. On the way to chow and on the way to the library, in the library, as my attention drifted from *The Sound and the Fury*, I realized how I'd misunderstood Sergeant Russell's grievance. The "Harry" he'd first referred to when he spoke of betrayal I'd assumed as a correspondent in an adulterous affair with his wife. But the sergeant was not divorcing his wife; he was divorcing the great love of his life, the Army. And it was former president Harry Truman, a man the sergeant had trusted, as Harry too, the sergeant claimed, had once been a member of the Klu Klux Klan; and yet it was Truman, the former Commander-in-Chief who gave the order for the mongrelization of the army, surrendering the military and society to miscegenation, and the rule of chaos. Corporal Bickford said that it was NCOS like Sergeant Russell who made the Army work. Sergeant Russell shrugged and said that he couldn't be persuaded to reenlist. He calculated the benefits he would receive as a retiree after twenty rather than thirty years, and said he'd live reasonably well. He hoped his papers were processed promptly so that he could be on his way by the end of the month, "Before Captain Jefferson the new CO, a colored, assumes command." Corporal Bickford commiserated. He apologized for the former president since he too came from Missouri, but the corporal said in his own behalf he hadn't voted for Truman. And the corporal glanced at me as someone who was complicit in Truman's rise to power.

I'd seen that look of recognition flash in the corporal's eyes before. Corporal Bickford was billeted in the same barracks where on weekends I visited Bruce and Gabe with my record collection of the Norman Granz's jazz concerts. Gabe's military occupational specialty named him a cook, and he did make meals at the Mess Hall palatable. Gabe was also an aspiring musician/composer and he played trumpet, piano, bass, and guitar. I'd heard Gabe on guitar; he was wonderful. Bruce who worked at the Quartermaster claimed that he had played alto saxophone until he'd heard Charlie Parker and gave it up. Now his

51

ambition, once he completed his three-year tour of duty, was to become an entrepreneur of the new music, to help make it known all over the world.

In the blessed corner of the barracks, the portable phonograph on the floor, we listened. There wasn't much talk. Sometimes there was discussion and Gabe and Bruce could articulate something about the music they wanted a greater understanding of, Bruce demonstrating an aspect of his question by scat singing. I throbbed on the periphery. I'd confessed to Gabe that the music we listened to had provoked an impossible dream of fluency from which I'd never escape. Bruce smiled and said, "Yes." He quoted a composer whose name I've forgotten and said, "Music expresses what can't be expressed in any other way."

The evening Corporal Bickford passed by our corner on his way out of the barracks and paused, staring for a moment, we were listening to Thelonious Monk. Gabe played an invisible piano in accompaniment. We laughed as helplessly, as mercilessly as children hearing the endless innovation that beggared the word lyricism. Listening to Monk I laughed, trembled, heard a song being discovered again and again in every note, songs inside the song, music inside the music. As the music moved and shook us and I felt a nakedness, my eyes rolling in my head, I had a notion of the devout and frenzied prayer my father had fled on his way to Marxism. My laughter, Bruce's laughter, Gabriel's laughter hadn't been meant as mockery. Corporal Bickford had stopped for a moment and watched us. My eyes swept his face, Bruce and Gabe also looked in his direction. The laughter that shook us inside out wasn't a vindication, or celebration of the arrival of the new company commander who was approximately of the same dark hue as Gabe and Bruce. The corporal was certain we were laughing at him and that I was in league with something indeed dark. I couldn't think of any way to explain.

After pay day, on Saturday nights, once a month, I sat alone in the enlisted men's club, drank and preached temperance to myself. My silent exhortation like the other languid thoughts journeying through my mind, each thought having the authority of magic, carried the danger of an imperative I had to obey, the sensuous mental life a seduction

I couldn't resist. I don't know whether my preaching moderation was responsible for keeping the binge a once-a-month occasion that became a fortnightly necessity years later, but I also felt a great democratic surge, a powerful urge toward universality, and when I got into a couple of scraps, the cause of which I never remembered, I did remember a joyousness that lingered even the morning after. I could find as a solitary drinker a larger embrace of humanity.

The windows that ran around the enlisted men's club filled with the bay of Inchon, ocean, clouds, sky of stars and riding moon swirling like the rings of Saturn, as inside, at the center I journeyed an otherness that almost made me a regular guy, comprehensible to the others. The morning after, days after, I would hear theories about the cause of the scraps I'd been in and I didn't know which to credit; but I was happy, and the theorists offering explanation seemed happy too. But there were also in those nights moments when I was a kid again, and I knew how one cowardly act can require numberless acts of bravery as I saw myself again leaping from roof to roof.

Sergeant Russell's papers came through. He would be shipping out, stateside, within a week. The remaining days were filled with awkward farewells. Various troopers came up to Sergeant Russell, clutched him, shoved him, Sergeant Russell clutched and shoved back; they shook hands and thumped one another on the back. Sergeant Russell's repeated farewells to Corporal Bickford cautioned that now that the corporal was no longer charged with ministering to the sergeant's hangovers the corporal might be tempted to pick up a drink, in which case the corporal was likely to capsize his life, lose a stripe, possibly find himself in the stockade; and the sergeant said it would behoove the corporal to find a new standard operational procedure for his duties to keep him on track and away from trouble. Sergeant Russell said to Corporal Bickford "Nothin' so bad that a drink won't make it worse."

Master Sergeant Keating would assume responsibility of the Motor Pool under the aegis of First Lieutenant Flood. Sergeant Keating was a short round man with a permanent air of preoccupation. He loved nothing so much as the automobile engine. People were interesting in so far as they could be compared with the workings of the engine.

When Sergeant Keating walked across the Motor Pool floor on his way to confer with Sergeant Russell and Corporal Bickford his hands reached out to touch affectionately the fender of a Jeep, the hood of a truck.

Sergeant Keating's misgiving concerning Mr. Kim's clairvoyance in locating a malfunction in a vehicle engine persisted despite Mr. Kim's record of accuracy. It was, for Sergeant Keating, the process he objected to, some sort of magic, intuition given as dark largesse to be paid for later with malaise, one's soul losing some portion of light. The only thing that would do was the moral and step-by-step labor to diagnose and correct the malady as thoroughly as possible, fondling and studying each part of the machine with the care of a lover discovering the mystery for the first time. What was scientific was humble, constant labor, prayer.

Sergeant Russell and Corporal Bickford discussed Mr. Kim and me as I stood close by. Sergeant Russell had reassured Sergeant Keating that we were anomalies he needn't worry himself about. Sergeant Russell spoke softly. Corporal Bickford raised his voice, glanced in my direction and said, "a numbnuts fuck up." Sergeant Russell said, "Naw, more like an old hound goin' deaf, he ain't entirely bad." I said, "I heard that." Sergeant Russell and Corporal Bickford laughed and applauded, as if my response were proof of some remedial progress achieved by my proximity to them. Sergeant Keating studied me with a look of resignation: I was something he'd never be able to fix, and he didn't want to waste his time trying to figure out how.

Mr. Kim loaded the metal cabinet that was part of Sergeant Russell's office onto his back, bending low, lifting his chin so that he could see where he was going and went off to deliver it as directed to headquarters. When I moved to assist Mr. Kim, Sergeant Russell commanded, "As you were, trooper, don't interfere with the man's job of work."

Mr. Kim wore an L-shaped frame on his back and had ropes that lashed the metal cabinet to the frame; the ropes tied at the center of Mr. Kim's chest, he grasped the ends of the rope. Bent forward, the cabinet jutted out a couple of feet past the top of his head. He made his way forward across the littered floor. I thought I saw Mr. Kim limping. His progress across the floor strewn with barrels, tires, tools and the carcasses of two vehicles awaiting resurrection made Mr. Kim's movement herky-jerky, like a man traversing a tight rope, about to topple any moment. Mr. Kim's right foot trembled in air and sweat ran down his impassive face. I followed him across the floor; I would catch him if he fell. The two sergeants and the corporal laughed as the gravitational force of Mr. Kim's labor pulled me in his wake.

Mr. Kim made his way through the Motor Pool into the shed where the worn and spare tires were stocked and where the Korean workers took their meals; the GIs complained that they couldn't stand the stench of kimchi, a dish consisting of pickled cabbage, peppers and garlic. The troopers claimed that the stink, like the rank smell of the honey buckets of human shit that the Koreans hauled to fertilize their rice paddies, made them ill. In the shed Mr. Sung came up alongside me, bowed slightly touching my elbow so lightly that if I hadn't seen him I wouldn't have felt his touch. "Please," he whispered. He clasped his hands at the center of his chest, lifted his head and gestured toward his throat where a crucifix hung. "I am new Christian," he said, almost one year." I said, "Yes." He said, smiling, "I see you study Mr. Kim, good for you, Mr. Kim number one." I turned losing sight of Mr. Kim who had progressed out of the shed. When I turned back to Mr. Sung I saw that he had again picked up the broom that was almost always in his hands. Mr. Sung, a thin man, perhaps in his thirties, seemed to sweep incessantly, the broom might have had some force of its own which propelled him into peripatetic circles around the floor as he spoke. Mr. Sung's face bore an astonishing resemblance to Buster Keaton's, although the droll melancholy of the Keaton face was more than mitigated by Mr. Sung's mobilizing his cheeks, mouth, and eyes into the appearance of happiness. He swept in a circle around me that grew wider, accompanied by smiles and bows, but I was kept within the center of his orbit.

The other Korean worker, Mr. Shin, had finished eating. He was young, handsome, powerfully built, and his habitual silence seemed a means of keeping his anger in check. I found it unnerving to look directly into his eyes. I'd learned that he could speak English, but rarely did; when he had to speak, he spoke in Korean to Mr. Sung or Mr. Kim. He'd finished eating and was looking down a well of stacked truck tires. He spoke frugally, his silence massive.

I began to understand. Mr. Sung and Mr. Shin were concerned with losing their positions. They knew of the change in command and didn't know what it would mean for them. Mr. Sung finally asked if I would speak in their behalf. I said that I would and tried to explain that I lacked the authority to determine the outcome, and I doubted that the changes in the chain of command would affect them. I think Mr. Sung interpreted my statement as a reluctance to speak in their behalf. Before I could reassure him he invoked the name of Mr. Kim. "Mr. Kim's words are spoken to persons of all ranks from his heart to the hearts of all," Mr. Sung paused with the broom for emphasis. He looked at me, took my silence for acknowledgment, resumed sweeping and said, "Mr. Kim is householder who supports much family and any who arrive in our village and claim to be family."

Mr. Sung swept, his footwork exceptional. The sphere he made was accommodating, the diameter constant, he and his broom were always in front of me. I repeated that he was not to worry, I would speak in his and the others' behalf, and that it was doubtful that they would lose their positions. I danced to the right circling out of his orbit. Mr. Sung called after me in his sweet, importuning voice and said that Mr. Kim never acted out of a desire for gain, even spiritual, and Mr. Kim had told him that the world of nirvana and samsara are one.

On Sergeant Russell's last day his eyes shone with a benevolent light, the cigarette smoke he exhaled had the odor of bourbon, he stood ramrod straight in his freshly pressed and clean khakis, supervising the installation of Sergeant Keating. First Lieutenant Flood would eventually appear at the Motor Pool, look about as though his most fleeting glance gathered all and everything. He'd say "Good work soldier, carry on," and return to his life at the Officer's Club. Sergeant Russell continued to whisper cautionary advice into Corporal Bickford's ear. Mr. Kim had removed Sergeant Russell's desk and chair. He set up a seat for Sergeant Keating, instigated and insisted upon by Sergeant Russell, that was a sort of throne, a pillowed bench and back support atop of a four-sided ladder structure, the pinnacle from which he could observe all that was happening below him. Mr. Kim had fetched for Sergeant Keating, a pair of binoculars and a bullhorn. It was Sergeant Russell who knew where these items could be found.

When Mr. Kim returned to Sergeant Russell to see if anything more was required of him in setting up Sergeant Keating's place of command, I saw that Mr. Kim's limp was more pronounced. He locomoted forward bobbing up and down, the heel of his right foot touching the floor gingerly, he maintained his balance. He came to rest and waited for his next order. I looked down at the hurt foot that gave off an odor like meat going bad. The foot was wrapped in white cloth, soaked in some kind of disinfectant not strong enough to obscure the smell of the injury. Mr. Kim wore rubber slippers the GIs called "E.T.-WA" boots, which was pidgin that translated for the GIs and Koreans into "Come On Boots."

Mr. Kim stood still, a figure of unfathomable grace, his strength a mystery. His head could have been hewed from a rock, but the living eyes were radiant with a language I couldn't be sure I'd heard. But years later, before my body began to betray me, I considered that perhaps wisdom might be more than a default position.

Sergeants Russell and Keating and Corporal Bickford stood together holding their noses. Corporal Bickford said something about the Koreans disobeying orders and eating lunch in the work area. They laughed. Mr. Kim studied the men working and loafing, the two sergeants and the corporal clinking glasses and toasting, and beyond the roar of all the noise and the babble of the celebratory expletives he seemed to see into the heart of time.

On Sergeant Russell's last day the farewells, the various toasts with beer and bourbon, a greater disorder prevailed, work and party coexisting in a rowdiness that stifled the feelings a man found inconvenient.

I said to Sergeant Russell, "Mr. Kim's foot is injured, he needs medical attention." Sergeant Russell looked at me with a glazed, benevolent stare. I repeated, "Mr. Kim needs medical attention." Mr. Kim watched, the event interesting in itself. Resting on one of the lower steps of Sergeant Keating's tower was the bullhorn. I picked it up, put it to my lips and declared, "Mr. Kim's foot is injured, we must get him to the medics!" The pronouncement boomed throughout the Motor Pool.

Mr. Kim and I, with a resentful PFC Glidding at the wheel of the jeep, since neither Mr. Kim nor I could drive, were dispatched by Sergeant Russell, Sergeant Keating and Corporal Bickford. The cheering men regarded the jeep a ship of fools. Sergeant Russell was smiling beatifically, he no longer had a care.

It was a hazy, humid day. The jeep moved in clouds of dust. Mr. Kim, PFC Glidding and I, coated like relics, squinted. To my left through the haze and dust I could make out the forms of the women following the receding ocean, bending to retrieve what the retreating sea revealed. The spectral shapes of the women, filling the baskets tied around their waists, shadowed the ocean that withdrew toward the horizon, where the low-lying clouds marked the place the ocean would disappear.

Mr. Kim, slate gray in the dust, seemed to be enjoying the ride. He swayed. I watched him. His foot gave off a mortal stink. I had one eye closed and squinted through the other between the splayed fingers of my right hand, which I held across my face. PFC Glidding sitting up front drove and cursed. Keeping my fingers latticed over my open eye I turned to watch the ocean uncover itself on the way to disappearing as the indefatigable shadows of women rummaged in the mud for edibles.

PFC Glidding gripped the wheel and sped the jeep down the rucked road, a great cloud of dust enveloping us. Maniacal behind the wheel, at the top of his voice, Glidding testified that each month he sent his allotment check home to his mother, which she accepted as her due, without ever a word of appreciation. He had never done anything that his father found praiseworthy, and all the family's resources had gone into funding the lavish wedding for his older sister Gladys, then her divorce, and now Gladys's training in the college of cosmetology. And here he was chauffeuring "a gook and a misfit."

At the Motor Pool, just before we left, damn near everybody drinking, Glidding had protested the injustices he endured. Repeating himself, he interrupted Sergeant Russell's booze-fueled serenity. The Sergeant's glacial eyes lit and he said, "PFC Glidding, I promise, if you don't shut the fuck up I'm gonna take you by the windpipe and you'll find out if you can breathe through your asshole."

We arrived in front of the Quonset hut that was the medical center. Glidding slammed his foot on the brake, we lurched, bounced, almost launched out of the jeep. He hung on to the wheel, bug-eyed and loony with revelation. Mr. Kim and I climbed out of the jeep. "Glidding," I said, "We'll see you when we come out." He rested his arms against the steering wheel and laid his head on his arms. Encased in grit he too appeared a piece of statuary with incongruous human eyes.

At the side of the door was a spigot of water and beneath it a bucket. I turned on the tap. Mr. Kim and I attempted to wash the dirt from our faces and necks. We beat storms of dust from one another's chest, backs, slapped at our trousers. He bowed after I thumped clouds of dust from his chest and back, and I bowed to him after he did the same for me. We attempted to rinse our swampy heads.

Inside, the staff sergeant stood with a hypodermic syringe in his raised right hand at the center of some eight GIs seated in two rows on metal folding chairs. A few were smirking. The sergeant with the syringe pointed to a shelf of towels. The bald, stout sergeant built wide and close to the ground, cheerful and grim, spoke in the voice of command that is made and perfected in the realm where sergeants are made. His right cheek, ballooned with chewing tobacco, jiggled. "Mens!" he barked, "you had to play, and now you pay. However, you sorry-assed bastards who been warned but went to Chancre Alley anyway, well I'll stick you with a needle, but they's got shit there the docs ain't even catalogued. You better start thinkin' about how you're gonna say goodbye to your wives and sweethearts back home. Before you go deaf and blind you can take your Tough Shit forms to the chaplain for advice." The men stirred in the metal folding chairs, several laughed. The sergeant gripped the hypodermic like a dagger he was about to plunge into the chest of the trooper seated closest to him. The boy jumped from his chair, fell on his ass and looked up stupidly. The sergeant hollered, "You think I'm here for your entertainment! When I yell Ten Hut I wanna hear your pussies pucker! Ten Hut!" All but the trooper seated on the floor struggling to rise and one young trooper whose face had been stamped with a defiance made by everything that is not supposed to happen to a child, rose like a snake being charmed out of a basket, while the others came to attention.

Standing they looked like figures mined from a grotto, patinated in grime, sweat etching human lips and eyes in their faces, the sergeant's voice an anvil compounding an impossible-to-follow incantation of curses; polymorphous, enraged, the foul tirade seemed to pound the troopers into awe. "And you filthy sons-a-bitches march your candy asses outta here and clean yourselves up. Try to look like soldiers. Then I'll stick you with medicine."

They trooped outside. I heard water running from the tap. The sergeant looked at me, nearly saw me but I gained obscurity from standing next to Mr. Kim. The sergeant turned away spitting out residual curses, clearing his throat, the puffed cheek throbbing under his mad eye, a thread of tobacco juice drooled on his chin. The sergeant's thumb dabbed at his chin, flecked and endowed the air, a master finessing chiaroscuro in a vision only he could see.

In an undertone he chanted at the screen door that slammed shut behind the troopers filing out, "You shudda stayed home, but you left, right, left, right …"

Again I explained to the sergeant why I was there. I don't know what he heard. Briefly the cheek puffed with chewing tobacco paused, the sergeant still, concentrating. The ballooned cheek wobbled again and the sergeant repeated, "What are you standin' there for? You think you got something special?" For the third time I explained that I wasn't on sick call because I had a dose. That I might be claiming a malady that wasn't VD irritated him, a trooper coming on sick call with something he couldn't treat was a provocation. I said it all again in a soothing voice. The sergeant growled, "The Doc, Captain Martin ain't here, he had to haul ass to Seoul, a meetin' with the big brass. Come back tomorra." I pointed to Mr. Kim's foot. I said, "You can smell it, I hope it's not gangrene. He needs a shot of antibiotic and to get the injury cleaned up." "I tole you," the sergeant said, "I ain't authorized for that, and the gook ain't authorized personnel." "Mr. Kim works for us at the Motor Pool; at least give him a shot." The sergeant, in a state of disbelief because I was still standing there, arguing with him, looked from me to Mr. Kim. Mr. Kim stood still and watched. The raving sergeant might have been turbulent weather that Mr. Kim studied through a window. "Private, you can try tomorra, when the captain is here, now haul ass!" I said, "Please." The staff sergeant's white-hot face thrust close to mine. "There's a gook Red Cross station about a mile up the hill, now you and this kimchi-eatin'-piss-complexioned-dwarf double time outta here, or you're gonna need medical attention."

We walked. My strolling, Mr. Kim's leisurely limp taunting the sergeant, I could feel his heat on my neck. At the door I turned to say "Fuck you, Sergeant" and Mr. Kim shook his head no. I kept silent and the sergeant and I exchanged looks of such pure hatred that I felt exhilarated, oddly free.

I looked around. The jeep and PFC Glidding were nowhere in sight. Up the road in a swirl of dust I saw the back end of a bus, one of our two and a half ton trucks heading back across the causeway to the base. Now I was close to raving, but in the presence of Mr. Kim I restrained myself. He pointed in the opposite direction. "That way. We walk, not far. Maybe catch ride." Mr. Kim's limp was nimble. His seesaw motion propelled him forward at a quick march pace. I was not inclined to question his intention to walk. I followed Mr. Kim's hip-hop ascent up the road. I thought that we had probably walked a mile; no one passed us and there wasn't any sign of the Red Cross station.

The heat sweated the color out of the mountain, shrubs and rocks moon gray, the sun's heavy light pouring down, the color of pewter. The gradual climb required greater effort to continue at a steady pace, at least for me. Up ahead, about fifty yards, Mr. Kim, with the peculiar gait of a three-legged goat, made his way without pause.

When I was fairly certain that we must have walked at least two miles, perhaps three, I decided that I would ask Mr. Kim after we continued a while longer if he had any idea where we were. He continued on ceaselessly and I was ashamed to ask him to stop and rest for my sake. I wanted to make my inquiry after an honorable length of time.

The road was too narrow for trucks, perhaps a jeep could negotiate the road but its progress wouldn't have been that much faster than traveling on foot. The road could accommodate the small powerful Manchurian ponies and carts we hadn't yet passed. I wondered why the Red Cross would set up an aid station in so difficult a place to get to, but maybe the inhabitants we hadn't seen could get to the place on foot or hauled in a cart by one of the ponies.

We came to a turn in the road where there were two paths, one an undulating descent and the other veering off to the right that ascended. Mr. Kim waited for me. When I came alongside him he pointed to the ascending path. I nodded yes and we continued.

Alongside the rock-strewn path there was some shrubbery spawning in the inhospitable geologic strata, bordering the road the rocks imbedded in the ground were covered with green fungus-like stuff.

I began to think of the hike as an exercise in silence, saying only what was absolutely necessary. Beyond fatigue, I made my way cautiously.

I was thirsty. It hadn't seemed necessary at the outset to carry a canteen with water. Looking down into the bay I could see that the tide was in, the smoking glare of the sun had inched toward the west. I did recall maneuvers on similar terrain, with full pack and M-1 rifle when troops covered about two miles an hour, and given the tension behind my knees I estimated that we had probably been walking, climbing up and down for at least three hours.

The hot breeze became moist weight on my shoulders. Mr. Kim ahead and below me disappeared behind a great shelf of rock. The claw of a stillborn, leafless tree jutted out of the rock, each branch against the sky pointing in a contradictory direction. I called, "Mr. Kim, where are we?" If I wasn't able to keep up with him I'd be lost.

I skidded down an incline into a wider path. Ten paces ahead of me stood an old man, lean as a stick, his pony hitched to a wooden cart. The smell of human shit in lidded buckets tied with rope and packed tightly in the cart had preceded the sight of the old man and his toothless smile. His white beard, the threads of a spider's web, through which I could see the bony lump of his Adam's apple, rode up and down to the faint sound of his breath. On his head a hat like a sawed off stove pipe with a wide black brim. His white blouse and trousers resembled pajamas. He and Mr. Kim were talking. The small, broad, Manchurian pony stood harnessed to the cart.

Beyond the stink of the shit, the conversation between the old man and Mr. Kim went on and on, and I couldn't guess from the sound if the discussion was coming to a conclusion. The monumental head of the pony appeared composed of flies out of which looked the most humane eyes I'd seen in any creature. The pox of flies swarmed and buzzed around the pony's head. I looked into the immense eyes of the pony and waited.

The farewell went on and on. They were inordinately grateful for having met and although I couldn't understand a word I thought I heard some parting phrase repeated over and over, and watched a long series of ritual bows. Again and again they seemed at the point of parting but resumed the repetition of the same phrase and commenced another series of bows.

The old man on foot, the pony hauling the cart of honey buckets, a stream of flies hovering above them, they descended the path in the direction we had come. The smell lingered when they were no longer in sight. I turned and saw Mr. Kim sitting on the ground, his legs sprawled in front of him. I don't remember a discussion. The accord was present in my mind and I took Mr. Kim on my back. I bent low and helped hoist his thighs up over my shoulders. He held the sides of my head with the palms of his hands and sat up straight, his bottom centered on the back of my neck. His legs dangled past my waist. The odor of his injured foot rose to my nostrils. His weight tolerable. Still I was anxious. Perched on me, Mr. Kim pointed to the ascending path. The failure to transport Mr. Kim could be damning. I assumed from the dialogue I hadn't understood that the old man had reassured Mr. Kim we were headed in the right direction.

Hiking up and down, the slow grinding roller coaster ascent and descent over narrow paths terraced into a labyrinth. Mr. Kim on and above me made encouraging sounds. We came out onto a plateau. I could see the bay, the roofs of the Quonset huts that made up the base, and the causeway (built by American POW's during World War II) that crossed the bay to the entrance of the base. Looking down I had the impression that I hadn't climbed higher than the tenement roof I'd climbed as a boy in search of a breeze during a stifling New York summer.

The stones churned beneath my feet, Mr. Kim gained weight. As I trod the inconclusive journey my anxieties were honed into imponderables. What if Mr. Kim on my back was the weight of my shortcomings, the palpable moral weakness which I struggled under? And if I unloaded the weight would I lose even this truth and live a weakling's life of shabby illusion?

I was thirsty. My thighs were beginning to cramp. I paused for a moment. Mr. Kim's arm extended in front of my face, the hand with only the thumb remaining pointed to a horizon of mountains where the sky and the earth were separated by a white line of cloud. Was there something he wanted me to understand from the vision he pointed to? Softly Mr. Kim knocked on the top of my head with his knuckles. I plodded on. My temples throbbed, my knees and back stiff, hamstrings taut. I was afraid that if I stopped to rest I wouldn't be able to go on.

I stumbled, glanced upward and saw Mr. Kim extend his arms like wings, correcting my balance. I'd struggled beyond exhaustion. Now I was limping. Mr. Kim part of my back, like a hunchback's hump, the deformity belonged to me. The burning blister on the back of my right heel, a reproach.

My boots had never fit properly. I knew it would be futile to go to the quartermaster to exchange them for a pair that might fit. The quartermaster would hand me another set of boots that would be too large or too small. I would have to return to the black market. The boss, ancient Miss Sung was better stocked than the quartermaster. She would try to sell me booze, cans of Spam, a weary virgin of dubious provenance, and provide boots that fit. I turned my head, looked up. The faint moon sat on Mr. Kim's head in a sea of sky where the sun still reigned, leaking twilight.

In the near distance I saw something hoped for, unsure I'd actually seen it: a whitewashed dwelling with a tin roof mirroring oblivion. There was a red cross painted on the white door. A figure in a white smock flashed in a window and then I saw nothing. I tottered. Mr. Kim put his hands over my eyes and I halted. I felt him climb down, the separation, the sudden lightness disorienting, some part of me falling away. He was standing in front of me repeating, "No more carry." The hand with the four stumps and the thumb waved in front of my face blocking the window where I thought I'd seen a figure appear. "No," said Mr. Kim, "you must not lose face, not …" and his hands described a beast of burden. We limped toward the white house.

Doctor Park, the physician in attendance at the Red Cross station, knew Mr. Kim. The young doctor's greeting conveyed the impression that he'd been waiting for us to arrive. Mr. Kim said something in Korean. Overcome and grateful for having reached a destination that existed, I praised the immaculate facility and the view of mountains from the window. Doctor Park smiled at the unaccountable good fortune of the beautiful view. The young doctor and I, circumspect and in a tizzy, went on smiling and gaping at one another. Doctor Park looked to Mr. Kim for approval as he translated, as if Mr. Kim had the capacity to read the hieroglyphics of gestures and facial tics that revealed the gist of all languages. The more precise translation offered to me was a courtesy. Doctor Park said that Mr. Kim apologized for taking me on such a roundabout journey. Mr. Kim knew where and when he was likely to encounter his old friend on the road. His old friend was to arrange for his niece to serve as a wet nurse for a baby born in Mr. Kim's village who was of mixed race. None of the women in Mr. Kim's village were willing to nurse the baby, and the mother, formally employed in one of Inchon's bars, had disappeared.

Doctor Park said he would attend to Mr. Kim's foot. However, he didn't have any penicillin and asked if I'd be good enough to contribute to the purchase of some more. I emptied my pockets. He emptied his. He chose only American dollars and explained that there was a rumor that the military was about to change the appearance of military pay currency and there was a panic in the Black Market: only dollars were acceptable. Doctor Park dispatched a young boy to run the errand to the nearby Chinese ghetto where there was certain to be an ample supply of antibiotics. Mr. Kim stood on one foot with his eyes closed.

EXALTATION

Purgatory was located in the basement of the church. The walls of the oblong, windowless room were a jaundiced white. There were rows of metal folding chairs and a lectern at the front of the room. Clouds of cigarette smoke saturated the air, which also reeked of germicide. Behind the lectern, a blackboard. Sometime in the past the church had maintained a parochial school. Ben couldn't dispel the feeling that in this room, children had been fearful and punished. Men and women welcomed one another. At a coffee urn set up on a table in a corner, two men looking worn and penitent embraced. Ben remembered looking into the mirror that morning and becoming reacquainted with his face. The broken nose livid and bent, the left eye half hooded by the bruised pouch of skin. What could be seen of the eye suggested the contemplation of something the right eye, looking out at the world was blind to, and his right hand was swollen. It would be a week before he could close his fingers around a pencil again. He would never have come to an AA meeting if the judge hadn't made his attendance the condition for the suspension of the drunk and disorderly charge. At first, what he couldn't remember struck the judge as insolence and Ben was threatened with a contempt citation, and a longer stay in jail. He did remember the laughter, mocking laughter echoing down a flight of steps. He'd gotten to his feet, collapsed, and on his belly dragged himself upward. Anesthetized as he was, still the sudden pain in his hamstrings toppled him, and he tumbled down the stairs. He stood before the judge, the deep bruises on his thighs and shins ached. The judge, mentioning his youth, suspended the sentence on condition that he embark on the program that offered rehabilitation. Ben had sufficient presence of mind to thank him.

Released from court he walked toward the subway and parts of the night in question came back to him, but he wasn't sure. Sometimes his recollection of the nights bled into one another. He'd struggled to fit his key in the lock. Aware that he was drunk he looked at the familiar door and hallway, orienting himself. Yes, he was at his door. But he couldn't get the key into the lock. He heard footsteps inside and wondered who had broken into his apartment. The trio that materialized from the shadows at his back pummeled him and laughed. He lowered his chin, crouched, and let his fists go. He was aware that in other brawls he'd often felt joyous. Then he was bouncing, somersaulting down the stairs. At the bottom of the stairwell he managed to get to his feet, and marveled that he hadn't broken any bones.

He didn't know how much time had elapsed as the police helped him to his feet. He tried to tell them that someone had broken into his apartment. They didn't seem interested as they hustled him out of the hallway toward the curb and the patrol car. Several residents of the building had gathered in the hallway and they spoke excitedly in Spanish and English, but the police were no more attentive to the complaints of his neighbors than they were to Ben's insisting that a crime had been committed. Handcuffed, out on the sidewalk, Ben noticed that it was getting light. It had been dark when he entered the building. A large cop pressed his head down with sufficient force but half solicitously so he wouldn't bump his head as he was thrust into the back seat of the patrol car.

When Ben thought of purgatory he must have been mumbling to himself as the stout man standing close by began to answer him, spouting information and observation, spinning an odd context for what had been Ben's involuntary remark, something that had escaped like a moan. The man's bald head shone in the fog of cigarette smoke. He rocked in a prayer-like motion Ben remembered from a former life. The lilting sing-song of the man's voice turned every declarative statement into inquiry. Ben recognized in the man, who would introduce himself as Morris, a species of Jewish polymath he felt related to in some familial way. Morris said, "You won't find it named in the Bible, but in the thirteenth century the Roman Church officially recognized purgatory. It's not a synonym for hell, but a place of temporary suffering where one can expiate one's sins, get clean. Hell, according to ancient apocryphal texts is not south of us, but in the third heaven. Anyway, better to be in hell with a wise man than in paradise with a fool. No? How do you do, I'm Morris." Ben wiping tears from his eyes shook Morris's hand. "I know," Morris said, "you're not crying, it's the smoke."

At each meeting someone told the story of how he or she got there. Morris had introduced Ben to Jeff. Morris and Jeff, at subsequent meetings, told their stories. The three Jewish drunks had found one another, their camaraderie initiated upon hearing certain familiar inflections of voice and a related humor when describing catastrophe. Ben wasn't ready to tell his story. There were many parts he didn't know, absences when he'd been ambulatory for some portion of time, and afterward, no matter how incredulous, he was forced to depend on the accounts of various witnesses. The adventures and misadventures attributed to him were often plausible, and sometimes frightening. He listened for clues to what was his life. Often there was evidence beyond what acquaintances had told him: like the face he encountered in the mirror that he had to acknowledge as his own, as there was no one standing behind him. The battered looking cousin looking back at him, was him. After a span of days and an interval of weeks listening to the stories of others he seemed to remember more, pieces of his history all at once at hand. But the prerequisite for this recall required listening to the confessions of men and women in which, no matter how different the particulars of the narratives (or the narrators) Ben was able to identify his own insane imperatives.

The swelling of his right hand receded. When he sweated his perspiration no longer stank of booze. The blue swelling beneath his left eyebrow embellished the look of introspection. The welt on the bridge of his nose slanted down, like the short arm of a clock, forever fixed at five, the onset of happy hour at the bars in the city. If his nostalgia for the illusory freedom of not giving a damn became too enticing, he fished chocolate kisses from his pocket, peeled the tin foil from each chocolate, and jammed the fistful of candy into his mouth. Somehow the taste of chocolate mitigated the memory of the longed for first rush of a boiler-maker. The meeting began. The Christian drunks recited the Lord's Prayer while the Jewish drunks remained silent. Morris waddled over to Jeff and Ben, and the three, startled to find themselves alive and in the cellar of a church said in unison, "Nu, we're all here." "To have a synagogue," Morris whispered, "we need a quorum, ten adult Jewish males. But because it's not always possible to find the ten to make a minyan, exceptions are allowed, for instance a circumcision or a wedding. A wedding without ten adult male guests, would be maybe, a rush job at City Hall. We could think of this like a circumcision, no? A covenant to begin a new life? According to tradition Abraham circumcised himself. Sometimes you got to improvise."

When Ben was able to announce at a meeting that he'd gone thirty days without drinking he received applause. When he announced he'd gone sixty days without drinking he received applause and Morris asked if he'd tell his story. Ben said he wasn't ready.

Now there were days when Ben felt a calm as deep as intoxication. Selfish as a miser hoarding his wealth, he desired to talk to no one. He skipped meetings and was glad he didn't have a telephone. Neither Jeff nor Morris knew where he lived. Morris had said, "Not even the Angel of Death can scare some alkies. These are the low bottom drunks. They have to wreck body and mind before they die. You're lucky to have gotten here so young." Ben didn't feel young, or old. He felt himself concealed, hidden from time until the evening hours when solitude became desolate; he was not subject to the mere passing of the day, but the end of an era as every night he entered a new dark age. The one room apartment with the dilapidated armchair, convertible couch, bookcase, small table with a hot plate on it, and the bathtub with the door lid on it, which also served as his desk and occupied most of the kitchen alcove, seemed spartan during the day, and at night, squalid. On the bathtub desk was a typewriter and a pile of manuscripts. If he succumbed to reading what he'd written during the day, he found that the stories that had seemed the very tissue of his being were revealed at night as counterfeit, and he was ashamed. When he stopped taking night classes at City College and managed to get himself fired at the warehouse so that he could collect unemployment checks and have four unencumbered months to write, and read what he pleased, he'd felt that he'd committed a brave and necessary act. Even the first week of nights felt pretty good. But as he was overtaken with revulsion for the language he'd put on paper, he had to get out, not only to assuage his disgust, but to find some redeeming act.

Ben, taking to the street, fingered the six ten-dollar bills in his pocket. He walked past a liquor store and a bar without going in; the delay was akin to foreplay. The treasure of the sixty days promised that when he put down the first double shot of whiskey and the beer chaser the heat would spread through his chest, warming his heart and like the first time, he'd taste a levity that promised freedom. Whatever happened, events would have their own meaning and he could live there, if he were brave enough. Moreover, he might live again in the dream of eloquence he couldn't repudiate.

The ritual required the laying of a foundation. The next time he passed a liquor store he went in. In an alleyway between a tenement and a garage that was closed he drank the pint of whiskey. Now, when he sat at the bar, he could sip beer moderately and savor the "varieties of religious experience."

At the bar he decided to reinforce his foundation and ordered a double shot of Jameson and a beer chaser. Mickey the bartender stroked his gray mustache with his thumb, paused and said, "Kid, do yourself a favor and disappear." Ben wondered whether he owed Mickey an apology. He couldn't remember, but said, "Sorry for any trouble I might have caused." Mickey sighed. To Ben's left a comfortable six feet away there were two men still in their work clothes drinking beer and discussing how the welfare system, supported by the taxes of hard-working people assured that the lazy and irresponsible could remain lazy and irresponsible. At a table in a corner, adjacent to the bar, a middle-aged woman bundled in a winter coat despite the mild weather stared into her drink as if reading tea leaves. At a distance to Ben's right sat a woman whose attractiveness drew the attention of the other two men at the bar who agreed that if it were not for the idle poor they could be rich. Mickey replenished the handsome woman's drink and said, "Helen, I didn't forget," and dropped an olive in her martini. Ben became aware that as in childhood what claimed his interest left him staring, bereft of discretion. Looking directly into her eyes he had inflicted an unwanted intimacy. As though he were a subway exhibitionist flashing his nakedness, now in the glare of the woman's contempt, he lowered his eyes and she reached into her purse and put on a pair of sunglasses.

Ben bought himself another double shot of whiskey. He gulped the whiskey and sipped the beer. The heat the booze brought to his head was different from the inflammation the woman's hateful glance had brought to his face. Ben sensed that every man's fate gained glamour by simply being near her. Her presence gave momentousness to the evening. It was not merely time that had punished her beauty, but something else: perhaps innocent bravery, a capacity for taking on the world that revealed the paucity of what any man might offer. He wanted to tell her these things, tell her his appreciation, his gratitude. Now he was able to lift his head and look at her again; blameless he was moved by the need to make an honorable gesture. But the sunglasses masked her. Whatever she thought or felt was rendered opaque behind the dark lenses. Still, Ben thought he recognized her, felt that he knew her or had known her. He remembered anonymity expressed as a principle at the meetings. She like all the others would have offered only her first name, and said, "And I'm an alcoholic." And like Ben she wasn't quite ready to quit, she desired one more dance with the Devil.

Ben sipped his beer. He seemed to recall aspects of her story, although he didn't remember her telling it. He might not have been attentive, sitting in the blue fog of cigarette smoke, having heard so many stories, so many calamities. The narrators petitioning the "Higher Power" that they referred to obliquely, as the nearly dead were absolved of sectarian passion in the democracy of ruin. They petitioned in the hope that they could be restored to life. Ben suspected that he probably saw her there, perhaps even heard her speak at the meeting in the church on the Upper East Side where, it was said there was a better class of drunks and the men were required to wear ties. He was not likely to see Morris or Jeff so far uptown; they had presumed to know him, warn him of the alcoholic's egoism, and the dangers of terminal individuality. Ben decided that the way to convey his respect was to at least appear oblivious to the lady's presence.

Ben looked at the clock. Morris and Jeff would be at the meeting that began during the supper hour. Morris, Ben thought, was a surprise. He would never have imagined roly-poly Morris as a former marine. Yet when he told his story, Ben learned that he had survived the most savage fighting in the South Pacific. When Morris came home from World War II a decorated hero, he came closer to death in the celebratory chaos of an unending party than he had on Iwo Jima. Obliging Morris couldn't say no and it seemed that every inhabitant in the city wanted to buy him a drink. Before the war Morris had dreamed of being another Gene Krupa. Now he was a math teacher in a high school for gifted students. Whenever Morris, the aging bachelor, spoke at a meeting he concluded with a sincere and general marriage proposal to every unmarried woman in the room. Jeff was a very different story. He had been the major strategist for a congressman whose political philosophy made an essential claim on his conscience. But as the years wore on, the politics left Jeff bereft of himself, except for self-loathing. He readily admitted that he remained in thrall to the glamour of being so close to power. A handsome man, it was difficult for him to remember a time when he was not unfaithful to his wife. His capacity for analysis and rhetoric seeped poison into his blood, which he doused with the palliative of endless martinis. While Jeff sickened, the congressman thrived. Jeff's wife remained devoted to him; but when his teenage daughter expressed a deep and abiding contempt for her father, Jeff staggered into the program. Now he worked for the civil service. He spoke slowly and carefully, purging from his vocabulary any superlatives. He was constantly on guard against heightened language and studiously matter of fact. Ben had found Jeff's sobriety scary, a sort of inverted Faustian deal in which only devotion to the mundane might yield salvation.

Ben placed a ten-dollar bill on the bar. He'd planned to move on when he'd drunk that amount in beer. But as he'd begun to retrieve the events that would make the medium of time he could once again inhabit, he thought it best not to cut off the fuel for the enterprise. He swallowed a mouthful of beer, closed his eyes, and knew that he'd have to do what he'd dreamed. As he placed another ten-dollar bill on the bar Mickey leaned over and whispered, "You don't have to be a hero, and turn everything into fuckin' tragedy." Ben heard tenderness in Mickey's voice. The expression of concern touched him and he said, "Let me buy you a drink." The bartender said, "Thanks, not while I'm working." And so, to commemorate the moment Ben bought a round of drinks for the four patrons; three of whom raised their glasses by way of saying "thanks." The fourth, the careworn beauty keeping her eyes secret behind the dark lenses acknowledged no one, as Mickey topped her drink. Ben glanced at her and thought, she is a woman to whom evil things have happened. Perhaps the dark glasses provide respite from seeing the world too clearly. Awash in sympathetic magic, Ben willed something like hope, like prayer, in her direction. And it was then that he began to feel that even his failures were glorious, the striving a source of unending desire: the story he'd attempted to write (*The Adventures of An Autodidact*) and had judged a failure was still alive in him. Now a man of means, grateful, he was ready to hug everyone in the bar.

There was a shift in the population. A steady flow of men in suits, carrying attaché cases were arriving. The guys with lunch pails and thermoses were leaving, the bar had become crowded. The Friday night festivity felt more like New Year's Eve, something unruly and defiant in the celebration. Crowded as the bar was, the stool to Helen's right remained empty. Tiny meteors of neon light streaked across the dark lenses of her sunglasses. The patrons, except for the sanctuary of space surrounding Helen, were packed two deep at the bar. In addition to Mickey, a second bartender had come on duty. He was bald and massive with a Fu Manchu mustache that made him look like a wrestler who played the role of the villain. As he served martinis and Manhattans to the patrons on either side of Ben, Ben cried "A Moscow Mule." From somewhere in the bar another voice cried, "A horse, a horse, my kingdom for a horse," and there was laughter. The huge, quick bartender covered half the length of the bar, served drinks, returned, reached over

Ben's head and served the patrons standing behind Ben, and then set the Moscow Mule in front of Ben. He gulped it down. The bartender moved away toward patrons signaling with empty glasses. The mass of bodies squeezing Ben on either side ejected him backward and now he was standing behind the second row of drinkers pressing in toward the bar, and he had to take a leak.

In the lavatory that looked like a whitewashed cave, he took a long piss. He rested his chin on top of the tall white urinal and held on to the sides like a man clinging to a raft, adrift in the ocean. He rested for a while, and then made his way to the only vacant seat at the bar, next to Helen. She said, "The seat's reserved." Ben sat down, "I'll give it up whenever the party arrives." "You better be quick about it," she said. Close by, Mickey wiped the bar, and the man sitting in front of him said, "The greatest sacrifice I've made for my kids is not blowing my brains out, and God forgive me, I've resented them for it." "Al," Mickey said, "I don't start hearing confessions until midnight." Helen removed her glasses and studied the man. Ben wondered, was she the woman who had earlier in the evening, said, "Are you going to live your life like a drunken sailor so you won't be mistaken for Shylock?"—or had that happened another night, in another bar? Looking at her he was a little afraid. Did she see through masks, even the mask that said: here are the secrets of my heart laid bare? Helen was staring at him. He was startled. She was older than he'd thought, and more careworn, but still beautiful; she'd always be beautiful. The contrast between her pale skin and black hair was stark. The fine bones of her face and neck suggested that even in the construction of her skeleton, her maker had already intended her to be beautiful. But when the door to the stock-room and rear exit swung open and another bartender emerged, a fluorescent light splashed a glare over her head and shoulders, and for a moment Ben could see the crone peering through the face of the beautiful woman. "Miss," he said, "May I buy you a drink?" She smiled. "How can I say no, you're such a sincere boy, and you're still trying to say yes in a big way." Mickey frowned and moved toward a patron waving an empty glass. Ben, embarrassed, almost blurted that he was old enough to vote. The unspoken assertion made him feel ridiculous and he tried to remember and assure himself that during the two months that he'd attended AA meetings, he hadn't revealed much about himself beyond saying, "My name is Ben and I'm an alcoholic." Helen's voice sounded familiar and remote. It was a cultivated voice, the pronunciation crisp, the timbre grated with a cigarette smoker's huskiness. Could she have been an actress at some time? During the long evening he'd imagined Helen's life. He thought that years ago she had probably come to New York to study and become an actress. That hadn't worked out. She could have worked as a model. Then Ben remembered the two times he attended AA meetings at the church on the Upper East Side where all the fancy drunks went, and he had been required to wear a tie. A woman had told her story, and it was Helen's story. The woman had been forthcoming and defiant in her account of the things that finally compelled her to desire sobriety. For a long time, she said too long, she had worked as a waitress. She had also modeled in the Garment Center and worked as an actress; but she'd waitressed years longer than she had modeled or acted. "And oh," she said, "for a month I danced at a topless bar. The guy who owned the place figured I owed him favors. That's when I hit bottom."

Ben paused in his conjecture of Helen's life, embarrassed, as if he'd been prying and blundered into the truth. He'd also reached where he wanted to be. One sip less and he wouldn't have arrived. One sip more and he would have overshot his destination. He sat still. Perhaps he could fine tune the moment with the littlest of sips. Carefully, he brought the glass to his lips; the drop of beer lolled on his tongue and the moment opened: time a residence where he could abide, and he concluded that quite aside from the haunting sense of déjà vu Helen incited, they were, after all, strangers. Nevertheless, the feeling persisted that she was not a stranger. He swallowed and Mickey was there, in front of him, bending over the bar. "Ben, I been servin' poison for years, and you're one of the youngest, most far-gone drunks I seen." "Mickey," Helen said, "You're all heart." Ben emptied his pockets, putting his keys, wallet, a five-dollar bill, two singles, and seventy-eight cents on the bar. He figured that he could afford two more beers and a tip for the bartenders. Mickey poured beer into the glass he tipped expertly and placed it in front of Ben. He removed a dollar and some change, turned, rang it up in the cash register, turned again and scooped up the rest of the money, Ben's keys, and wallet and said, "Keep this in your pocket." Ben said nothing. Mickey removed a wallet from his back pocket, opened it like a book, and laid it on the bar. "Look at this." He pointed to a photo of a stout girl with a pretty face wearing a graduation cap and gown. "My daughter Mary, she's in law school, makin' somethin' of herself. It costs. You ever think about the future?" Ben thought *what if this is my last drink?* The notion was momentous and he looked at Mickey and Helen as if he'd already said "goodbye". Mickey picked up a damp cloth, wiped the bar around Ben's elbows and wrung drops of water out of the cloth that dripped into the sink beneath the bar.

"Hey," Ben said, to demonstrate he was alert and not as drunk as Mickey might think, "That guy's trying to get your attention." Mickey looked and quickly came out from behind the bar and elbowed his way through the crowd toward the man. Helen frowned. The tall, middle-aged man with white hair wore a blue suit, white shirt and white tie. He wasn't carrying an attaché case or waving an empty glass. Without effort, he looked over the heads of everyone at the bar and waited as bulky Mickey plowed through the patrons and arrived open-mouthed. There was something deferential, Ben thought, in the way Mickey bent his head to hear what the man was saying to him. Mickey had been nodding yes and smiling before the man had said a word. Helen, irate, slapped a ten-dollar bill on the counter, took her pack of cigarettes from the bar, and made her way to the rear exit. Mickey lunged after her. Midway, he stopped and turned. He made an imploring gesture with his hands and seemed frightened by the indifference of the white-haired man.

Mickey ran through the corridor to the exit door. Ben ran after Mickey. Outside the full moon illuminated the parking lot. Ben trotted in the maze of cars. He heard the wind carrying their argument down the pathway of cars. Helen yelled, "Go to hell." Ben chased after her voice, came to the end of the path, rounded the corner and continued in the labyrinth. The quarrel modulated, soft, loud, rushing on the breeze within the footway between automobiles. Helen said, "It's my night off, and I never do business from a bar." Ben spied the profile of a lunatic running beside him; his heart lurched, and he fell. On his feet again he recognized the guy as he looked at his reflection on a car window. He continued at a brisk pace. His forehead hurt. A fragment of conversation he'd had with Mickey months ago came to mind and all at once Ben hated him, because Mickey counted on a God who could forgive anything. The full moon cast an icy sheen on the roofs of the cars. Ben slowed his pace. He reached a place where the column of cars made a right angle and turned into that path. And there was a man staggering toward him, waving and shouting, "hello, hello," as though he'd been searching, for Ben, and was overjoyed to have finally found him. When they were face to face, the young man, disheveled and plainly drunk said, "I can't remember where I parked the fucking car," stumbled on and hollered, "If you find it give a yell, it's a new blue Chevy." The fading resonance of the man's voice caught in its passing other voices, a man stating calmly, "Bitch," and the woman's voice countering, "Bastard." Ben hoisted himself over the hood of a Buick, slid down into the next lane, and saw them at about the distance of a runner rounding third base, and headed for home plate. They appeared to be jitterbugging, Ben stopped; he felt like an intruder. With the searing clarity of an insomniac, he saw them from some recall of dread, recognized them not from their faces but the circumstance that locked them together. They submitted to the dance wearily, oddly graceful. Bull-like Mickey caught Helen's hand, drawing her to him, and punched her in the stomach. She draped over his arm. Ben bolted. He didn't know what he was going to do until he dropped and slid over the asphalt as though he were stealing home plate, the asphalt shredding his pants, taking skin. Feet first he torpedoed Mickey's knees and Mickey crashed face forward.

Ben stood panting, his ass burning. Helen's nose was bleeding and she was bent over clutching her stomach. Mickey rolled over and sat up. His face was a mess. Slowly Helen straightened up and wiped blood from her lips with the hem of her dress. Ben shivered in the mild night air. This had happened before. He couldn't remember the particulars, but knew that it had happened before, and the woman had said, "I'm a moral person, I believe in Hell." Helen walked to Mickey and kicked him in the head. He fell backward, his skull making an awful sound banging off the asphalt. He lay still. Helen said, "Get his wallet." Ben couldn't move. "Okay, Lancelot, I'll do it myself." She went through Mickey's pockets, removed his wallet, took the cash, and tossed the wallet.

She grabbed Ben's hand, tugged, and they were off. He was amazed at how fast she could run in high-heel shoes. She wobbled and reeled, never slowing her pace, and didn't let go of his hand until she'd led him out of the maze.

They walked in circles wheezing. After a time he was breathing normally. He saw the high-rise apartment house across the street. There was a canopy over the entrance. On either side of the canopy was a scrawny, invalid looking tree, leafless and trussed with wires to a circular wrought iron base. Most of the windows in the apartment house were dark. The isolated windows of light made him long for the snug life he imagined living inside. The night was inexhaustible. He was tired of his revel, surfeited with magic, and he wanted to rest.

Helen stood, her face thrust close to his, "You figure I owe you somethin'?" Her voice had shed all refinement. It was low-rent and ready for trouble. Ben said, "No." She said, "No is right," and took a step back. Her nose was still bleeding. She wiped it with her sleeve. She surveyed him from head to toe, and said, "I got to get away from this city, like right now. If you have any sense you won't go back to Mickey's joint, ever. Understand?" Ben nodded yes. She said, "I doubt it," turned and looked for a cab. Seeing none she walked away as fast as she could. Ben watched her. She was halfway down the street when she turned and hurried toward him. He saw her getting closer and thought he'd embrace her. She stopped short of bumping into him, and he thrust his hands in front of him to cushion the collision. Helen grabbed his hand, and pressed cash into it. "Remember," she said, "what I told you. Don't go back to Mickey's. He's an ex-cop and so are his partners. They work both sides of the street. Believe me, you're lucky you're still breathin'." She put one hand on his shoulder, balancing herself as she lifted the shank of her right leg behind her, reached back and removed the high-heel shoe and let it fall to the sidewalk. Then she removed the left shoe. He felt the warm impress of her hand on his shoulder, the weight of her resting on him. His guts swooped. He thought, how can she leave like this, after what we've been through? He thought he heard her say yes, though her lips never moved. He knew she was dispensing balm, condescending to him. This long good-bye had him close to blacking out. Then he remembered how anxious he'd been when he was fifteen, because he expected to die in a nuclear holocaust before he ever got laid. And she was gone, running down the street with a shoe in each hand.

He plodded home sick, but didn't throw up. His knees and ass burned. He walked the deserted streets and looked for a cab, now that he had money. He saw neither a cab nor automobiles, except for the cars parked at the curb. He passed two bars that were closed. It was ridiculous, but he still wanted her, wanted to differentiate himself from every man she had known. He reminded himself that she was available for a price. He didn't want to think about the defeats that had left her with a respect for money, and he called himself dumb for not offering her refuge for the night. She wouldn't take the chance of going back to her apartment. She'd probably go straight to Grand Central Station, or Port Authority. But he could have kept her safe at his place. Mickey didn't know his address or his last name. At his apartment she could have cleaned herself up, taken a bath. She would ask him for a towel. Perhaps summon him to wash her back. He would touch her. She'd consider putting his yearning to rest. But maybe their conversation would lead them to a place where she would tell him her story, and he would have to choose between that intimacy or getting laid. It was a difficult choice. After thinking about it long enough to have his agitation become an itch simmering near his crotch, he longed to give up this perplexity.

He staggered to the door of his apartment wanting to believe that Helen was inured to degradation, or there was something in her, in spite of all, that remained inviolable. He managed to get his key in the lock, pushed the door, and stumbled into the dark. Dizzy, he made his way to the large worn armchair at the center of the room and lowered himself into the chair. He leaned his head on the back cushion and sat very still. If he moved he'd spew all over himself and then he'd have to sit there and stink. He heard traffic moving in the street and water gurgling in the pipes in the wall. He thought it must be getting close to morning. But the window facing him remained dark. Sunk in the bog of the chair, he closed his eyes.

He opened his eyes. It was still night. He wasn't reconciled to what remained unconsummated between himself and Helen. He wanted to turn on the lights but couldn't get out of the chair. Inside an elevator cage he plummeted down the shaft and heard the guttural roar, knew the savage importuning that consumed every sound on earth. The most bestial histrionics barking from a human mouth. Ben could see between the bars of his cage the infinite bone white field strewn with howling infants, their heads cracked eggs oozing brains.

He awoke screaming. The apartment was dark. He was alone. He commanded the screamer to shut up. The scream became a child's nagging whimper. He was soaked, couldn't stop shaking. Awake in the dark he was no longer falling. If he could get out of his chair, he'd use the fifty bucks Helen had given him and get a hair-of-the-dog; hell, with fifty bucks he could buy the whole dog. Rémy Martin—why not? He sweat and shivered, and the here and now became the last peek at the story he'd been writing. The language was inadequate. He couldn't abide this failure. There was then no work for which he was suited. This being so, he was unworthy of love. On and on it went. He thought and thought. Reason, fear's accomplice, every iota of life's business a downfall. Bits of light speckled the window. The radiator gonged. He was ready for sleep. And as if he had known always that he could be acquainted with his soul only by journeying through the things of this world, he stumbled upon this, the most fearful thing, the portly Jew in his soft flesh, the most provisional of garments, waddling among worlds, one of God's comic adjectives, his face an overgrown garden.

Don Juan, Senior Citizen

The child called to him, and Don Juan became aware that he had been sitting for some time with his hand in his shirt, rubbing at the flaking skin on his ribs. They were talking to him. His daughter Gracia stared, waiting for him to agree. Don Juan composed his face as though he were listening and thought of Generosa. The little boy's voice called, more insistent, and Don Juan took his hand out of his shirt, buttoned it, and saw his grandson's face through the globe of water; the small orange fish with red fins darted back and forth across the boy's smiling face, and the peanut-sized mermaid, the fish half of her silver and luminous, the tiny bosom looking like real flesh in the shimmering depth of water, floated up under the boy's eye. "A present for you, *Abuelo*," the boy said, and placed the fishbowl on the kitchen table. Don Juan's children, grandchildren, and various relatives crowding the narrow kitchen applauded. The boy stood very still studying his grandfather's face. Gracia asked "*Verdad?*" Don Juan pursed his lips, not knowing whether what Gracia was asking was, or was not so; all the while she talked he had been away sitting on a park bench with Generosa looking at the East River. "And see," the boy said laughing, "I have no spots." Don Juan looked at his grandson's brown, handsome face and remembered. The boy had just come from Puerto Rico that year and had never seen snow. Don Juan told Angelito that the icy white flakes would bleach white spots in his skin and Angelito had been afraid to go out and play in the snow. "See," said Angelito triumphantly, "No spots," and Don Juan embraced the boy.

Gracia looked to Don Juan once more to settle the dispute. "*Verdad?*" she implored, and then turned to Doña Gregoria, also called

Titi, or Tapon, and nodding vigorously vindicated Titi-Tapon's point of view. "Yes, it would have been an offense and an indignity," she said, "to have Toto lie in his coffin as Rosa had wanted. He was a drunkard certainly but ..."

Don Juan thought *Ach, otra vez*, again and again we must dispute the preparation for the wake of my brother Toto who has been in the ground over a year now. Don Juan knew he had made a mistake when he agreed to accompany the ladies to the Jewess's and serve as a translator. Gracia's English was sufficient, and he was not needed. But then Don Juan remembered that it was not really the matter of translation. He only wanted to get away from the corpse of his brother and the stench of the apartment. Toto had died of uremic poisoning and smelled very bad. Rosa, Toto's wife, Gracia and Titi-Tapon set off within minutes of Toto's passing, and the priest's arrival, for old Mrs. Feinstein's on Orchard Street.

When the four arrived, Mrs. Feinstein, bobbing and weaving in the doorway of the shop, gave up hawking at the passing crowd. Mrs. Feinstein, swifter than Western Union, could divine, from the harmony of her battered senses, misfortune moving down the street.

Gracia translated for Titi-Tapon; the old woman was very tired from the long vigil of the previous night. Don Juan assumed the attitude of a mere bystander and examined the merchandise in the shop with great interest. The first transactions were conducted in whispers. A new suit was purchased for Toto, and a white shirt, tie, and alligator shoes. Then Titi-Tapon said they would have to buy Toto new socks and underpants. Rosa said yes to the socks as Toto could not be laid out in the silk-lined coffin in the splendor of his blue serge suit with an expanse of naked ankle peeking out from between the tailored cuff of his new trousers and his alligator shoes, but the underpants seemed to Rosa an unnecessary extravagance. Titi disagreed. Rosa claimed that as Toto's widow her judgment was final. Titi laid claim to transcendent authority as this was also a religious matter, and it would be unseemly to send Toto off into eternity in his new suit without underpants. Rosa repeated that she was the wife and widow of Toto, the finality of the statement whistling thin menace through her flexing nostrils. Gracia arbitrated between the two. An elderly gentleman, his white head capped in a woolen skull cap, and wearing a military overcoat of World War I vintage with a medal pinned to the lapel, rose from behind a mound of trousers, stroked his bony chin and said, "Please, you should excuse me ladies, but the dead have rights too." Mrs. Feinstein, prodding a customer with whom she had just completed business out of the store, turned to the old man and said, "Morris, you want the suspenders? Yes, no, hello and goodbye."

The old man disappeared behind the mound of trousers. Gracia reminded Rosa that after all it was Titi-Tapon who had the account with Mrs. Feinstein and Titi who would pay. Titi screwed her face into displeasure; after all, her concern went beyond any material consideration. Gracia genuflected and suggested that perhaps she should go back to the house and return with Toto's sisters for a discussion with all those concerned. Mrs. Feinstein sighed, the three black rubber raincoats hanging from a wire above swayed in a breeze. Rosa screamed. Titi-Tapon got down on her knees and prayed. Gracia, at the top of her voice, so that she could be heard above Rosa's wailing and Titi's praying, reiterated as fairly as she could both Rosa's and Titi-Tapon's arguments. The old man's head popped up over the horizon of stacked trousers and said nothing. Rosa's eyes, spinning toward milky blindness, were fixed on the trinity of black raincoats floating above her, stately and judicial dark angels, their heads made of dust motes and lint. She whined: on the last day of his life Toto had staggered out of bed, snuck up behind her and kicked her so hard "that her ass sprung open like an umbrella." Propelled across the one room flat, Rosa in passage grabbed from the gas range the saucepan from which the water for tea had boiled to steam; the bottom of the pot was incandescent red and she banged Toto over the head with it. And now Rosa explained to the angels that the back of Toto's head was as bald as the blister on the palm of the hand with which she had grabbed the handle of the pot. Whatever the possibilities of Mary's infinite mercy Toto should not be mistaken for a monk because of his recently acquired bald pate. Despite his monkish appearance Toto had never renounced his bestial pleasures; he was what he had always been, a drunk and a fornicator.

Mrs. Feinstein said, "*Oy, oy.*" Titi-Tapon hurriedly concluded her prayer and from her knees said that there was still not sufficient reason to send Toto off into the next life without underwear. Rosa began to talk in tongues. Titi reminded Gracia that despite the yowling gibberish coming from Rosa's shuddering lips, Rosa was not a Pentecostal, but a true and lifelong Catholic. Mrs. Feinstein said, "*Oy, oy.*" Rosa said, "Arf, arf, meaow, Jesus, dezuzuzu." Mrs. Feinstein, thumping her bosom, commiserated with the suffering of women, and especially mothers, she swayed and shivered, her pudgy hands rising from the shelf of her bosom to disparage the thought, and announced "No," she would not, could not charge sales tax, five percent off for the grief of the world, and the underpants they could have wholesale.

Gracia looked across the kitchen table and waited for Don Juan to comment. He had heard it all too many times and said that the disorder in which Rosa, Gracia and Doña-Tia Gregoria had participated was the result of the loss of male authority, a problem endemic to North America. Gracia and Titi-Tapon exchanged long suffering glances, and Gracia reminded Don Juan that Rosa was not at his party. Don Juan said, "It is of no consequence." Gracia praised Mrs. Feinstein as a peacemaker and philanthropist. Titi-Tapon chided Don Juan's grandson. The boy was standing absolutely still, his black eyes wide and bemused staring into his grandfather's face. Gracia shook Angelito's shoulder as though trying to wake him from sleep. Angelito was six years old and neither simple nor backward. "Abuelo," he said, "you look like an old monkey"—and in the instant caught his lower lip in his teeth.

Doña-Tia Gregoria, whom Don Juan had nicknamed many years ago "Tapon" the little cork, because when Gregoria walked she bobbed up and down like a cork on the water, frowned; the pink tip of her tongue flicked out at the thin wisp of white moustache on her upper lip as she reached over to rap on the boy's head with her knuckles, as though courteously knocking at a neighbor's door, and she said, "*Boy.*" Aunts, uncles and the boy's father, Romero, applauded the knock-knock on the head, and Angelito's cousins laughed and chanted, "*Cocotazo,* Angelito got a *cocotazo.*" Don Juan rubbed gently at the top of Angelito's head and could feel heat coming from the boy's face. Don Juan leaned across the table where Titi-Tapon sat surrounded by three of Don Juan's daughters, and their children, two small ones sprawled on laps, three more charging around and in between the kitchen chairs, (two fathers stood behind the chairs puffing clouds of cigar smoke into the air and sipping rum). "Titi," Don Juan said to his ancient sister-in-law, sister of his first and principal wife, gone now, almost ten years, "Titi," Don Juan said, addressing her as the family always had since Doña Gregoria never married was mother to all, and thus called "Auntie." "Titi," Don Juan said, "do not chastise the boy, it is only that now we are old and worry too much about our dignity." Titi shifted her weight in the chair, folded her arms across her large bosom, and began to swing her feet which did not reach the floor. "Besides," Don Juan said, "I have seen and I do look like a monkey." A daughter, perhaps a granddaughter, a female relative certainly, the voice was of a grown woman, shouted something from beyond the beaded curtain where a phonograph played as the young people danced and the floor and walls throbbed, plates and cups stacked on the shelf above the sink shivered and chimed, the pipes hummed in the wall and a bead of water trembled and gleamed from the mouth of the faucet. The children ran about, and the tiny ones crawled on hands and knees. Those standing and eating from paper plates at the far end of the railroad flat (the bedroom was being used as the main dining area) felt the music quiver through feet, flesh and bone, and beyond the beaded curtain where the dancers danced, the young female relative of Don Juan called, "Popi, you are still handsome" and everyone cheered.

Then they disagreed about Don Juan's age. He said seventy-nine, Titi said eighty-one. Don Juan knew what this controversy was prelude to. Titi-Tapon, bobbing in her chair, would remind him once again that his Cuban girlfriend was, at fifty-five, too young for him, and that she (his Cuban *novia*, always Titi emphasized her Cubanness in hope of arousing family support) was only considering marriage to Don Juan in order to gain American citizenship; moreover, in Titi's judgment Juan was a fool to be signing his Social Security checks over to "that Cuban lady." She, the Cuban lady, was called Generosa, and Don Juan thought her well named. Juan thought whoever named Generosa was only commemorating how God made her, and although Juan did not believe in God, he considered that whatever power made her may have had some other purpose in mind than Juan's delight. Still when Juan thought of Generosa's legs (*ay*—if those are the roots can you imagine the potato) he was very happy.

Juan stared and saw that Titi's face, clenched into a look of unctuous command, was only one face. The kitchen filled with people, the three rooms of the railroad flat like a train that had barely averted a wreck and had stopped suddenly forming a loose and sloping Z through which funneled daughters, sons-in-law, sons, daughters-in-law, grandchildren, nephews, nieces, grand-nephews, and grand-nieces, all the faces flooding toward him, looking, expectant, so that the claim Titi's face made was, if not lost in the multitude, greatly diminished. Through it all he could make out the back of his daughter Gracia who had attended very closely his argument with Titi and counted, her lips laboriously computing his age as she fumbled and dropped the blue candles she had been arranging on the three-tiered cake. A child sitting on the floor at Gracia's feet happily chewed on a mouthful of the blue candles and Gracia looked down and shrieked. Don Juan laughed, and Titi's face, a replica of perfect contrition marred only by the curling wisp of white moustache, loomed once more into prominence.

Don Juan contemplated then what might be Titi's claim to saintliness. Not that he had any use for, or need of, saints; but Titi's charity marked time, reckoned years, and measured his life's passing. Her service was an aspect of catastrophe which included birth as well as death. She could assuage pain and cool fever; midwife, healer, gifted comforter of the dying, she'd arrive, death's dwarf-like emissary, hauling her paper shopping bag loaded with herbs, enema, rosary beads, and crucifix. There were times when Don Juan wondered whether it was death's small mercy or if mercy begot death in some manner he could not understand; but he had to acknowledge that among the many children she had saved, one many years ago had been his, and of course there was her care of Chaga, Don Juan's unfortunate and now middle-aged daughter. He did not want to think about that, or any of Titi's intimate services. But here she was, presuming to instruct him once again, her upper lip rising to reveal the scientific marvel of teeth purchased second-hand from a lady on Ludlow Street. The teeth almost fit. Titi kept her right hand to her mouth and through an intricate strumming (the articulate fingers never rested), mashed her food efficiently and spoke in slow deliberate cadence, the sound of the askew, ranked teeth clicking as each word stepped forward. She said, "Don Juan, you ..." And in between her words Don Juan said that at eighty Titi's memory had begun to dim and she could no longer be relied upon to remember anything beyond which funeral to attend. Titi genuflected. A hushed moan went up in the kitchen, groaning uncertainly among the riotous harmonies of timbales, dancing feet, laughter, squalling children, and the plumbing singing in the sweating walls. After all it was Titi's largesse that had made the party possible, and the party was meant to celebrate Don Juan's eightieth birthday. Don Juan heard the timid groan that had gone up and knew it was a reproach of sorts and thought, remorse has never been one of my emotions and I will not learn it now. And he could see as well as the others through the memory of waiting and waiting how that week, as so many times in the past, Titi in preparation for this event travelled underground through the stone bowels of the city in and out of trains, (she spoke no English and even if she had pride prevented her asking instruction) and a trip from the Bronx to Lower Manhattan that should have taken twenty minutes to a half hour became a journey of four hours; or when, as on this occasion, a complex distribution of bounty required many destinations, and the odyssey lasted two days.

Titi travelled the convoluted routes known and charted in memory that took her to far away Long Island and round back to the Bronx, Yankee Stadium, down to the furthest reaches of Brooklyn's swamps, Canarsie, and Chinatown; Marco Polo and Cortez had not seen a greater variety of humanity than Titi: the pink-fleshed bearded Jews in black gabardine, the grey Americans carrying leather boxes, turbaned Hindus, the new world black Muslims in the most immaculate white. Chinese wearing silence, and Hispanics and Africans attired in the best of purple raiment to be had at the bazaars of Fourteenth Street; all,

all, getting on, getting off, the shuddering, screeching, iron beast of a train. Titi sat, rolled, pitched forward in a half sleep, endured, her thick ankles rimmed in the tubing of her rolled down black cotton stockings, the ankles held propped between them the paper shopping bag laden with provisions: six codfish cakes, twelve saltine crackers, a thermos of *café con leche*, a canteen of water, two oranges, rosary beads and crucifix. All this lay on a folded white linen sheet, and beneath the sheet at the very bottom of the shopping bag, piled like leaves that had fallen from a tree, one thousand dollars. The thousand lay in a crisp bed of one hundred five-dollar bills upon which five hundred single dollar bills were rolled into little balls. The singles rolled into pellets and quantities of the fives tied in pink and blue ribbons made discreet distribution easier. Everyone in the family knew Titi had "hit the number," no one knew for exactly how much, but as always when Titi "hit the number" there was the odyssey with destinations in Brooklyn, Bronx, and Manhattan, where she would slip fifty into the pocket of a coat hanging from a door knob at Cecilia's, a hundred under a tablecloth at Neftali's, twenty in a medicine cabinet at Gracia's; the singles rolled into pellets were left at the bottom of fruit bowls, coffee pots, folded into diapers, rolled under couches, fistfuls stuffed into the freezer compartments of refrigerators. The traveling and dispensations would continue until the last dollar was gone. The anticipation among the family whenever Titi "hit the number" led to happy bedlam, celebration, or in the instances of crisis, reprieve.

Always Titi would hide the money and never tell how much she had hidden, or where. Sometimes weeks after her departure from a household, Gracia or Roberto and Cecilia, pressed by a particular and urgent need, would ask Titi if indeed they had found all she had left as they were behind on the rent, and Titi would resolutely refuse to divulge how much and where she had put the money. No amount of pleading, or screaming, could persuade her. And as Titi hit the number, two, sometimes three times a year, the family, often enough out of need and always in the desire to celebrate a perpetual Christmas, searched under mattresses, dragged furniture, ransacked closets, so that all, grownups and children, lived in a titillating disorder that promised now a new pair of shoes, television set, bottle of rum, sweets, and celebration. This endless hunt for what would translate into the unexpected new suit created a kind of random hope, a drowsy optimism that issued from Titi on her knees praying to Jesus.

Titi, at prayer, swayed on the callused knobs of her knees before the white candles. Crouched, silent, she knew when she saw Jesus above her, pinned to his Cross, his human aspect suffering, that she was right. The sign, his sign to her, his chin falling on the bony chest that heaved the barest sigh in the candlelight, was the nod that said, not only, yes the world is near its end, as so many of the faithful knew, but yes and yes to her, and the mortification of her flesh, and a nod of yes to her fidelity to Him. She, Doña Gregoria, who had never asked anything for herself, heard on these occasions a hushed and muddled whispering in her ear, a configuration of numbers that was promise and a clue to the dimensions of eternity. And that perplexity of numbers she sorted as she read them again burning on the refugee bookmaker's arm. During the many years Yudi Bloom had never charged Titi for placing a bet; she in return, and as courtesy, distributed the roll of tickets with the numbers on them (la bolita, this too carried in the paper shopping bag), and collected Yudi's bets among those friends who hailed from her hometown of Rincon and lived now in the projects on Prospect Avenue in the Bronx.

Titi, who had seen every Christmas and Easter the Mexican-made film version of the Passion play, knew that only a pharisee would equate playing the number with vice; the relationship of this activity (as with Bingo at St. Theresa's) to gambling was only apparent, and if the deity was a Jew, cast in recognizable human form, maybe his racial descendant, the refugee Yudi Bloom the Bookmaker in his white almost transparent skin, back bent as though at some time it might have been burdened with wings and face as beaten as the fourteen stations of the cross into permanent and irrevocable grief, might also be a fallen seraphim or angel.

Titi-Tapon and Yudi Bloom negotiating of a summer's day, hands flying, grunting, cooing and stamping feet, communicated beyond any confounding of alien tongues, the Tower of Babel transformed to a rude and magisterial dance of such power and grace Titi knew that sometime they caused rain; they moved in a circle over the sidewalk and knew that theirs was one of the more felicitous understandings in the world. Yudi hopped about in his iron-toed shoes and said, "Ya, ya" meaning yeah, yeah, and Titi called him Mr. Jeh-jeh. "Jeh Mr. Jeh-jeh," she said, nodding in the affirmative. Yudi, Mr. Jeh-jeh, laboring at speech, sweat pouring over his bald head, his eyelashes white with salt, heard from his own mouth a zoo of grunts that fetched a beatific smile from the small bouncing Spanish lady. Thus encouraged, Titi's voice gurgling "Jeh, jeh" sounded to Yudi like one of the birds of paradise, birds Titi could see on Yudi's short sleeved summer shirt, a flock of rainbow-colored doves aimed in flight at heaven. As Yudi's emaciated arm pointed up she read the burning numbers on his arm and was finally able to delineate the secret arithmetic Jesus whispered in her ear, which became the gift to Don Juan, the splendid party in all its accouterments, even to the roasted pig Don Juan could see through the kitchen window smoking among the pots of geraniums on the fire escape.

The three-tiered white glazed cake with the flames of too many candles, each candle with its trembling small light; the cake like a mock cathedral floated in Gracia's hands toward him and Don Juan turned away to look out the window. The pig's white eye stared back in bewilderment out of its roasted head, black flies buzzed between its blood red ribs, the sumptuous wreck of cooked flesh sat on the fire escape which was his daughter's garden. From the deep pail at the pig's blackened snout, a single stalk of corn grew, and there were boxes of tomatoes, green and red peppers, wooden cheese boxes with coriander and oregano, pots of geraniums, yellow roses; green vines curled around the iron bars of the fire escape and hung down in festoons that swayed in air above a clothesline flapping white bedsheets.

All shouted *"Feliz Cumpleanos"*; the happy birthdays and laughter roared in Don Juan's ears. At his feet he could feel a child crawling, and without looking he reached under the kitchen table and gave the little one a slice of cake. He could hear the happy sound of the child chewing. The phonograph in the next room grew louder. Overhead a parakeet began to squawk in its cage. An old grey cat with one blind eye padded softly on the edge of the sink and studied the bird with his good eye. Between the one eye of the cat and the pig's smoked marble of an eye looking in through the kitchen window, Don Juan sat surrounded by his children, grandchildren, nephews, nieces, grand-nephews, and grand-nieces, crowded to the very edge of the kitchen table. He recognized most of the faces, but confused their names, and he often could not remember with which mother he had had which child, and he was glad his memory had its own purposes. Out of the music and noise and the shrieking of children single words and phrases droned in his head. "La overtime," "el landlord," from these he inferred their lives and grew drowsy. He looked at the pink wall where the calendar with the picture of blonde blue-eyed Jesus pointed at his heart in flame, and Don Juan thought, *Judio loco*, I am a rational man and there are too many living things in this house. Titi announced, "You will never marry that Cuban lady." Don Juan saw and understood, the devout Titi would never utter a menace, only she shrugged with the weight of her omniscience, and repeated, "You will never marry that Cuban lady." Despite the warm day Don Juan felt a chill at his back and remembered five years ago the pneumonia that almost killed him. Titi had nursed him then and said, "The bad weed doesn't die."

Don Juan slid forward in his chair, reached behind him and took hold of the braided leather cord that ran through the wooden handle of the short machete that dangled from the knob on the back of the chair, and hung it around his neck; the blade reached his waist and felt cool through his white cotton shirt. He said, "Goodbye, I go home." His daughter Maria said, "Popi don't go." Don Juan said, "Enough party," stood up and found that his right leg had fallen asleep. He swayed for a moment, the numb leg tingling, Gracia came forward and put a slice of cake in his hand. He said, "It is time." A young man with a handsome, clean-shaven face, which Don Juan remembered vaguely as possibly his own, fifty years ago, asked, "Popi, you still live in Korea?" Don Juan looked at the young man and knew it was not one of the children he had had with Doña Gara, and he did not recognize this one as part of the brood he had with Consuelo. "Viet-Nam now," another said. "Oh, si," Don Juan said, remembering that the area of Lower Manhattan where he had lived the past eight years was considered bad and had been named variously after the places of famous wars. Don Juan stood and could feel his leg coming back to life. He wanted to be gone quickly, before any of his daughters suggested yet another time that it might be good if he lived with them, or that he ride the senior citizen's bus to a center in Greenwich Village where he could meet with friends and play dominoes; this advice he found ridiculous since he had taken down the one mirror in his apartment and had no desire to go to a place where he could find affinity with all that was bent, old, and ugly.

He moved forward stiffly, the slab of cake in his left hand, cautious and slow as a man walking in the dark. There was much shouting and crying against his leaving but his children, grandchildren, sons, daughters, daughters-in-law squeezed together making a path for him. It seemed to take a long time to reach the door and he fixed his eyes and kept nodding his head to acknowledge farewells and ward off embraces. The parakeet squawked above him. Trumpets blared from the phonograph, and the good-byes rained on his neck.

Finally he was beyond the door and in the hallway. It was possible to see in the many-layered dark. Through a density of sewer gray, Don Juan saw a few arm lengths ahead a large, locked opaque window, spotted with dead flies. He advanced slowly, right foot, then left foot joining right foot, before continuing down the steps, one step at a time; the habitual caution of his movements carrying him through the dark. He sniffed the aroma of frying oil, garlic, a sharp elixir above the stench of garbage and cat piss. He could still hear his party going on, laughter, the mention of his name and Generosa's among the sounds of many radios and televisions, murmurs, and low growls of domestic disturbance along with calls to the supper hour, and the pitiful shriek as of a child being dismembered, which after a moment he recognized as the nuptial combat of two cats echoing through the shaft of the unused dumbwaiter. He thought of Generosa and saw nothing for a moment: all the sounds melted into the equivalent of silence. He continued his slow steady descent toward the street. Tomorrow, he thought, tomorrow he would see her.

Don Juan arrived at his door breathing like a man who had just been saved from drowning. His life banged between his ears and the thudding blood made his eyes ache; his right knee was stiff and his feet burned as though recently thawed from a great freeze. Once inside, he secured the two locks, the chain, and the special police lock with the long metal pole that extended at an angle from inside the metal-sheeted door, down to the floor. On the way home he had looked behind him many times, more concerned with being followed by Titi than the muggers. He shuffled through the ankle-deep surf of crumbling newspapers and passed the large stuffed chair leaking coils of cotton wadding. The floor was completely covered with the accumulation of forty-five years of newspapers, left by the previous tenant, an old recluse named Shaumus Reardon O'Reilly, who was discovered dead one morning on the couch Don Juan lowered himself into. Don Juan liked having this extension of his "library" under foot. Lying on the couch he could reach into the crumbling newsprint and scoop up the bombing of Nagasaki, the atomic mushroom cloud fragile in his fingers dissolved into flakes and snowed down near Stalin's face, fading into the sea of alphabet; a mouse dropping like a leech on Josef S's cheek. On the wall beyond the couch a line of cockroaches migrating to the ceiling filed by a yellowing calendar which read "Season's Greetings, 1950, The Ace Plumbing Company, 747 Broome Street." The picture on the calendar showed a naked blonde woman wearing a Santa Claus hat patting her buttocks and winking. Beneath the Ace Plumbing Company calendar was a small shelf upon which sat a hot plate, its long frayed cord dangling to the floor, and Don Juan's library. The two hefty tomes, Spanish editions of Karl Marx's, *Das Kapital* and Victor Hugo's *Les Misérables* listed precipitously to the edge of the shelf. Don Juan sank into the rank smelling couch, the pain in his foot ebbed and he looked accusingly at the old gas refrigerator that he suspected had (through Titi's voodoo machinations) incubated in ice, the affliction of his feet. He felt the need to relieve his bladder but the toilet in the hallway seemed very far away and Don Juan stirred himself to reach for the chamber pot under the couch.

The relief was delicious; a glorious light flowed through the one window and Don Juan felt that after the hour it had taken him to climb the five flights of stairs he had earned this brilliance. He stretched out on the couch. The last light of the day penetrated his closed eyelids and released a constellation of red bubbles that floated up and then sank down to darkness. Don Juan remembered that he had forgotten his grandson's gift of the goldfish and the little mermaid. The small spheres of sinking colors went away. The dark was soothing.

Then it was light again. Brilliant, vivid, sun-filled light. When the old woman sitting on the bench waved to him, he was not alarmed; Don Juan knew he was only dreaming, and if the dream claimed any consequence he would tell the old woman that it was only dreaming. As the old woman came closer Don Juan realized that it was Doña Gara, as she had been at the end, except that she was smiling. She called to him across the expanse of empty beach, "Juan," she called, "I will see you soon, quite soon." But when they were face to face Doña Gara was the young beautiful Gara and she was not interested in Don Juan's protest. He said, "What are you talking about, woman, I feel fine. I'm in the best of health." The beautiful young face of Gara was immobile. The sea hummed and the voice of old Doña Gara living in his ears whispered, "I'll see you soon." Don Juan was shocked by the beauty of the young Gara and felt once more the violence of wanting her. The wind coming off the sea blew music through his fragile old bones only he could hear. Her face remained a mask. The music stopped and old as he was, Don Juan was again in the warfare of their early marriage. Now as then, he was as incapable of saying it as crying, and he felt how when she let it happen at all, his desire had to become her enterprise and his manhood was annulled. If touching was initiated by his passion she struggled and suffered as one suffocating and they were never equally naked. In spite of all they were profoundly married and silence concealed nothing. Gara's mask-like face answered his thoughts, "And how is my sister, your daughter, poor Chaga?" she asked. *Poor Chaga*, he thought, *born a repository of all the world's madness and mine*; still he did not, would not, believe in remorse though the life of Chaga (by way of Titi) followed him as relentlessly as Inspector Javert pursued Jean Valjean for the theft of a loaf of bread. Yes, in the first year of their marriage, he had gone from his wife's bed to his mother-in-law's bed, and back to his wife's bed. It was foreordained, thought Juan. Hadn't he, like so many of the young men of the village, looked forward to earthquakes? The earth shook, and people fled to the mountains. He stood among the cheering young men, coconuts like severed heads flew through the air, the ground trembled and heaved and he and the other young men waited for the moment when Gara's unconscionably beautiful mother would run out of the house in her slip.

The earthquakes would come, the inhabitants of the town fled to the mountains as their homes collapsed in heaps and the graveyard spewed up the dead. Refugee men, women, and children scurrying away with possessions piled on their heads and backs ran in one direction, away: they passed the young men, running in the opposite direction toward the house of Doña Angela, mother off Gara. The ocean would recede beyond sight, and in the air fish and birds were tossed like so much debris. The flying trunks of palm trees decapitated roofs and the church steeple; while those young men who dared, stood in front of Doña Angela's trembling house, the earth shuddering through their bones as they waited for the moment when she would run screaming out of the house in her slip. Only after that moment, cheering and dancing on the swaying, heaving ground, only after dancing around the barefoot, near-naked Doña Angela would the young men abandon the town. Doña Angela enjoyed her life ruthlessly and without regret, and Don Juan thought how in consequence, Gara's sister Gregoria, the old women of the town, and the priest, made of beautiful Doña Angela's beautiful daughter, Gara, a thing of virtue.

Doña Gara's frozen resolute face asked wordlessly, "Does my sister, your daughter, speak in a human voice or still make animal sounds?" Don Juan was about to answer that Chaga was as well as could be expected, cared for by Titi-Doña Gregoria, and yes Chaga often spoke in a human voice and no longer needed to be institutionalized; but when Don Juan spoke, he was young again, swinging in the hammock behind their house, in the first year of marriage, and he answered Doña Gara as he had then, saying "Yes, woman, your life is a masterpiece of penance."

Don Juan awoke from sleep and was aware that all that had transpired was only a dream, nevertheless he continued to argue with his first and principal wife Doña Gara. He was willing to admit that he carried many aches, pains, and maladies, but he was, fundamentally sound, and a man. Doña Gara's saying she would see him soon was only more of her usual provocations. And why, he shouted at her, why did you take to wearing black so young? Here he tasted bitterness; certainly there was no end to dying relatives, but young Gara taking on the color of mourning forever.... How apt a revenge and humiliation. See, world, see how the wife of Don Juan never recovers from mourning. And his heart hurt and his chest was tight. Don Juan heard his voice shouting at his wife, his voice like Doña Gara's voice in the dream, a thing in itself living in his ears, echoed and became the sustained shriek of the police car siren in the street.

He lay still and rested; the police siren indicated that the night had progressed, yet he felt he had not been sleeping long. Don Juan estimated that he had slept several hours, he could not know exactly; in the matter of clocks he felt almost as strongly as about mirrors; he would not tolerate some mechanical thing's ticking away in concert with the laboring muscle of his heart, the remaining hours of his life. He breathed deeply and the constriction in his chest passed, and he smelled the strong odor of the chamber pot beneath the couch. He rose, shuffled through the crackling newspapers to the darkened window, and emptied the chamber pot wishing that the stinking stuff falling down to the street would land on the junkies, and those of the young who had acclimated themselves so well to the way of junkies, that they too hunted old people.

Don Juan returned to the couch. He stretched out, rested his head, and thought of the various women in his life. He retained the names of several; Doña Gara of course, his wife of always, Gara a diminutive of Margarita, and the mistress of his middle years, Consuelo, meaning in English consolation, and she was. Don Juan recalled that he had several children with Consuelo, still it seemed a light thing and what he remembered of it most strongly now was that when they were in conflict Consuelo's weapon was disorder. The rooms of furniture were constantly rearranged, drawers of clothing, tools, even places for keeping food constantly rearranged, nothing would have a fixed place.

When vexed, Consuelo inflicted disarray and finally misplaced Don Juan. One morning Don Juan was searching for his pants and his guitar. Wandering about the house he encountered Consuelo's new lover. The new lover was searching in the larder for a piece of cheese and found Don Juan's pants. The two men confronted Consuelo. She laughed and they laughed and the laughter dispensed consequences. But tomorrow, he thought, tomorrow I see Generosa.

They had spoken of marriage. It had been many years, more than ten certainly since he had seen the *peluda*, the place of the woman's hair. He did not know if his desire was real, or a thing of the mind only; even if it was a thing of the mind only, it was very strong. And if Generosa was loud, a person of the street, she did not sell favors commercially, and most significant she was not put off by his appearance; a fact which Don Juan found most impressive on those occasions when, passing a store window, he was suddenly confronted with his reflection. That the wizened and balding old monkey blinking at him from the window contained his spirit was shocking, and unseemly. And, thought Don Juan, miraculously, the lovely and foul-mouthed Generosa is not put off; although in the tales and gossip Titi brought to his door, concerning Generosa, there was much that was discomforting, and the last that Titi brought was the most disturbing.

Don Juan had not let Titi in to tell it. He had considered not answering her knocking. Finally he made her speak through the narrow breach of the barely open door. The thin chain that held the door locked divided Titi's face, the links of chain running across where her eyes would be. She asked to be let in. Don Juan said no. Titi said something that insinuated and mocked his fear. Because of the way Titi had to conduct her false teeth as she spoke, Don Juan could not entirely understand what she was saying, but he surmised her argument, and as she pitched herself into a sentence he knew she would never complete, he fashioned a response. Among other things he thought she said "Chee-na" and so he brought an orange and handed it to her through the narrow opening. She shook her head no and told him once more that she was not the one who had put his socks in the refrigerator. Don Juan said, "Ach, old woman that was six years ago," as though it really didn't matter. Titi nodded yes and as her head bobbed down her eyes became visible beneath the links of chain and he could see her look of triumph. Titi swallowed and now her face took on an expression of solicitous concern. Don Juan resisted the impulse to strike her and said nothing. Discussion, he was sure, could only add to her strength, as she would remind him that she was a good Catholic and that he ought to know she would never do that kind of thing. Still the memory of it made his feet ache and burn all over again.

He had reached into the freezer compartment of the refrigerator, groping for a pork chop, and came out with his frozen sock. He smashed the gleaming ice-foot whiskered with snowy spicules against the wall; the shattered pieces flew about the room. Don Juan bent down and picked up a fragment that was stinging cold to the touch; within the transparent, jagged fragment of ice, was a small photograph of Millie Gonzalez. The face of the widow Millie (short for Milagro or miracle) looked up, grave and diminutive from the palm of his hand, embalmed in ice. Don Juan, then a widower of four or five years, and the widow Millie Gonzalez, had planned to live together as man and wife. Millie, amazed, had said, "I don't feel right." He held her hand, but Millie's loneliness had become impersonal and vast, and she said, "Also my throat itches." He said, "Don't worry." She said, "Juanito, somebody is interfering with me, Juanito, some person of ill will has written my name in a black book." He put his arm around her shoulder and speaking as one old joke to another said, "Nonsense, woman," and brought Millie a bag of oranges. Millie's nose began to run. She said, "I heard talk." Don Juan told Millie of the two great lights in his life— *primero* Carlos Marx—and also Victor Hugo who wrote the grand story of Jean Valjean hounded all his life because of the theft of a loaf of bread. He talked to her of the need for justice in the world, and reason and science, all of which Don Juan explained did not preclude the foremost necessity, the need to wage life heroically. Milagro caught a cold. She wanted to know who was responsible. Don Juan beat on his chest with his fist, and said, "I take responsibility." Don Juan caught Millie's cold. She got better. Don Juan's cold became pneumonia. Millie said, "Goodbye, old man. Somebody in your voodoo family seriously does not like me, you talk like a communist, and I am too old for this much kind of troubles, *adios.*"

He almost died. Titi took care of him. Through the haze of fever he asked Titi not to trundle him off to death. She smiled, demure, modest, and pressed the stinking poultice to his forehead. Don Juan shivered under the bedclothes and his teeth chattered. Titi whispered that she was keeping Doña Tara's gravesite in order and that her sister, his daughter, Chaga was very much improved; and she reassured him that "the bad weed does not die."

Titi, wedged in the narrow opening of the partially opened door, spoke, shrugged, and intimated that she had knowledge, a revelation concerning Generosa that perhaps he could not bear. Don Juan speaking on his side of the door chain assumed disdain and told her to say what she had to say as he had important matters to attend to and could not spend his day seriously entertaining an old woman's gossip; *chisme* he called it, the most trivial form of chatter. Titi informed Don Juan that since he was the widower of her sister, Doña Gara, and Doña Gara's virtue had always been beyond question, as he, and all the world knew, she Titi had some concern for his dignity, and that his taking up with a woman of the street—not that she, Titi, was without compassion for those who had been touched by life, and even had some history, but there were limits, a bottom beyond which was unspeakable filth and certainly eternal damnation and she knew for certain from a reliable source that his *novia Cubana* Generosa had lived several years with—she lowered her voice and hissed, "a Chinese merchant marine, Chinese," she said, "*Chino,*" and handed back to Don Juan the orange he had given her through the space of the barely open door. Don Juan said, "*Muchas gracias,* Doña Gregoria" and closed the door softly in her face.

When Don Juan asked Generosa about it they were sitting on a park bench, fifty feet from the East River, facing the Brooklyn side. It was a hot day and a group of little girls played a game in which they took turns hopping on one foot into squares, drawn in chalk on the pavement. From time to time one of the little girls would yell, "Potsy." On an adjacent bench a woman rocked a baby carriage. Seagulls swooped down out of the cloudy low hanging sky to feast on the garbage in the river. The factories on the Brooklyn side boiled in a fog that made it possible to imagine them fortresses in a lost city of another time. Generosa waved a fly from her nose and Don Juan thought how graceful and fine-boned her hands were. The metal bracelets on her wrists chimed and this gave him pleasure. He sighed and again asked her if it was true that she had lived with a Chinese merchant marine. Generosa cleared her throat. She had a deep, gravelly, almost mannish voice, which at first Don Juan had not liked, but now found oddly exciting. "Chinese?" she asked. "*Si, Chino,*" he reaffirmed. She turned so that she was facing him and said, "Do ju know why the Chinese got slanty eye and bucked teeth?" As Generosa said this she stuck her upper teeth out past her lower lip and squeezed her eyes into slits; the face with narrowed eyes and protruding teeth insisted, "Well, do ju know?" Don Juan noticed that the little girls had stopped playing and were staring. He was embarrassed and answered by shaking his head no. Generosa said, "It's because they do this so much," and Generosa's hand went to her lap and grasped an invisible penis; pumping up and down, her face as she masturbated the invisible penis, went from her own recognizable face to blank innocence, and as the make-believe rapture increased her eyes narrowed to slits, her upper teeth protruded, the whole face squeezed into a look of frantic and oblivious idiocy. The mother on the nearby bench rocking the baby carriage had been watching over her shoulder. The woman jumped to her feet, screamed a warning in Polish or Russian to the little girls playing potsy and fled. The woman ran pushing the zig-zagging baby carriage in front of her, and she did not look back. The one little girl standing in the chalked square on a huge pink number three, one leg bent behind her was the first to laugh. Then the other little girls laughed. Generosa, eyes dead level with Don Juan said, "Anything else ju want to know, honey?" her gravelly voice commencing in a mellow alto and sing-songing down to resonant baritone.

Don Juan exchanged the deflated pillow behind his head for the fat one at his feet; he readjusted the sharp angles of his body on the soft and giving couch and thought, truly the woman has a mouth like the trapdoors to Hell; but holding her delicately made hand is a fine thing. He thought how Generosa had let him feel her upper arm, and various rounded places of her body, and although he could not be sure that his desire was actual, he had felt a stirring and perhaps he would have once more, a married life. He saw that the night which lay on the window bore no resemblance to the rich twilight and the fine day that had passed; the dark was starless and steamy as the stuff that smoked up from manhole covers. Don Juan preferred not to see it; the dirty mist, which seeped in under the window sill, made his chest hurt. He closed his eyes but did not want to let himself go into that depth of sleep where he would meet Doña Gara again. He had become quite adept at migrating through various levels of sleep, at drowsing, resting, and reflecting at will, while holding himself comfortably away from that realm of sleep that would deprive him of his waking life entirely. He lay there and thought of the island, and that was very pleasant. It would be wonderful to go back again with his bride Generosa, but the time of the midnight "cha-cha flight" from La Guardia which cost only sixty-five dollars was long gone; now, the fare would require a very large sum of money. A sweet breeze wafted in from the East River. He sank deep into the soft couch and was confident that he would not drift toward the dream that had left the imprint of the mountains on his vision. He remembered the weather on the island, how the sunlight tasted of salt and how at midday the white cement walls of houses were doused with buckets of water and looked like steaming cakes; and in the simmering drowse of siesta everyone's door was open and silence a balm, and those swinging in hammocks all shared a variety of sleep. Under the natural sovereignty of the sun the temper of the day was benign, and the heat bearable in the humble artifice of a trance. Don Juan thought that if he stayed here he was likely to meet Doña Gara again, but he was not prepared to leave, and when Samuel Gompers, white as a ghost, stepped from behind the palm tree and tipped his straw boater in greeting, Don Juan was glad to see his old friend again. Sam chided Juan for sleeping on the couch with his shoes on. Juan sat up, removed one shoe and rubbed the arch of his foot. "Good," said Sam, "Here's a cigar, only don't smoke in bed." The two admired the landscape. The goats grazed on the hill that sloped down to the beach.

Don Juan peeked behind Samuel Gompers to see if Doña Gara was hiding there. Samuel thanked Juan for providing protection when he, Juan, and the century were young. Samuel Gompers had come to the island to inform the sugar cane workers of their rights. Juan remembered and said, "It was not necessary to shoot anyone," only once he had fired his shotgun in the air to warn those who were about to toss the brimming bedpans from their windows. Nothing extraordinary, only politics as usual. Don Juan felt obliged to explain why he was no longer a *revolucionario*. He said, "Señor Sam, it is not so much a matter of age." The great labor leader lifted the straw boater from his head and wiped sweat from his brow. Señor Samuel seemed not particularly interested and stared off toward the ocean. Don Juan, a little disconcerted by his old comrade's indifference and the sense that Doña Gara was near, listening, and mocking, felt nevertheless compelled to justify himself. Don Juan explained that he was no longer a *revolucionario* because many of his grandchildren and great grandchildren were Americanos, the blood was mixed but still his. In the pigment of their skins he could recognize his own "ink," and he would not make war on his own blood. Samuel Gompers said nothing and presented a light to Don Juan's cigar. Don Juan puffed on his cigar feeling foolish. He could hear the derisive laughter of his grandchildren and great-grandchildren coming from a nearby bush; the laughter orchestrated, he knew, by Doña Gara. "Wait," Don Juan called out to Samuel Gompers, who had tipped his straw hat and walked off. Don Juan ran to the resplendent laughing bush, each leaf illuminated by the sun echoing children's laughter. Don Juan reached into the bush and seized a child's hand and pulled. The little hand was anchored by a small and deft weight; something bounced here and there on the other side of the thicket. Don Juan readjusted the purchase of his feet and tugged at the small brown hand; the struggle shook children's laughter from the bush and when Angelito came tumbling out he seemed about to cry. Don Juan wanted the boys as witness, to corroborate that he, Don Juan, had instructed Angelito against the false capitalist teaching that all principles necessary for the flourishing of life would issue naturally from the swine trough of commerce, if only no one interfered with the pigs. Don Juan was about to say, tell him Angelito, tell Señor Sam what I told you, but he saw that Señor Samuel Gompers had wandered off far to the horizon; and Angelito, suppressing tears, accused his grandfather of leaving behind his present of the goldfish and the mermaid.

Angelito stood with his back to the green bush and stared at his grandfather. Don Juan trying to remember what he had not attended to, heard Angelito say "fish," and thought the boy was recounting the story Don Juan had told him of the earthquakes. Don Juan saw the look of grievance on Angelo's handsome face, and held fast onto his grandson's hand, marveling as though his own fate had been invented that very moment in the form of this brown and nimble boy.

Angelito said, "The snowflakes did not bleach spots into my face." Don Juan said, "Yes of course." Angelito said, "You meant to frighten me with that story, Abuelo." "No, *hijo*, only to make the opportunity to prove your valor by playing in the strange phenomenon of snow." Angelito's face slowly ventured a broad smile and Don Juan opened his arms and embraced his grandson. The sunlight shining through the top of the palm tree lighted up Don Juan's old shabby chair, with its coils of cotton wadding drooling from the arms and back; the chair breathed and beckoned like an old friend. Don Juan sat down in the chair, and Angelito climbed into his lap. Angelito put his hands, which were cold and wet as they had been the first time he had seen and played in snow, to Don Juan's cheeks. The two laughed and shivered and in the crab-like tangle of their embrace the wet became warm. Don Juan thought, this happened in waking and so it is not something born of the dream alone, and knowing this pleased him; he felt his will was not entirely absent from what was happening. Angelito snuggled in his grandfather's arms, and as he had before, said, "Grandfather, soon, before Easter and Good Friday, I will take First Communion." And the two enjoying the repetition of performance like actors honing a single gesture to its ultimate perfection, smiled discreet, nearly invisible smiles. "Good Friday, eh," said Don Juan, "I told you a false tale of snow, now I will tell you a true tale of false blood." Angelito, as he had the first time he heard it, rested his head on his grandfather's chest and closed his eyes. "Remember," Don Juan said, to his grandson, "how the

Island is in spring; this was a spring of long ago. Your mother was a little girl then, and her sisters, and your grandmother tiptoed about so as not to arouse the attention of the devil who was loose since the tormented Jewish ghost languished once more on the Cross." "*Diablo,*" Angelito said into Don Juan's chest. "*Si,* the devil," said Don Juan, "and Good Friday is the name they gave it, and many on the Island were out to make the most of the opportunity the devil provided. Such was the custom based upon the belief that during the benighted hours of Christ's agony on the Cross, the outrage of Don Jesus's innocent blood spawns an anarchy in which cuckolds may seek revenge, and thieves steal; every crime has license in a world under the devil's dominion. The pious and the women pray, and keep a vigil waiting and praying, praying and waiting, for the return of beloved Jesus. During the hours of the agony until *Sabado de Gloria* when Jesus ascends and his presence is again felt on the earth there is the praying and devotions of the pious. But meanwhile, during the hours of the agony, *el Capitan* of police may assuage the ache of his existence by beating his wife, and one is free to do violence to one's neighbor with impunity from the law. It is a custom as necessary as Christmas for those who need it. And I," Don Juan explained to his drowsing grandson, "and the goats grazing on the hill were among the few reasonable creatures on the Island."

It was, he remembered, a fine day. The sun was bright and the heat not oppressive; the clarity of the air made everything seem a special feast for the eyes. Don Juan lay in his hammock swinging gently between two trees; turning he could see, through the open window of his house, Doña Gara and his daughters moving furtively. He turned away and looked to the top of the hill, where the church, rebuilt since the last earthquake, was draped in the colors of mourning. The church shrouded in the huge hanging drapes and bunting of black and purple, the belfry incongruously shaped in the black wind billowed drapes, appeared ludicrous to Don Juan under the bright and indifferent sun. He breathed deeply of the perfumed earth and knew that in part his wife's religiosity was revenge, (although her piety had taken on a power of its own) and when he was unable to laugh, he suffered rage. He could not in truth understand her moral imperatives any more than he could understand the necessity of doing the wash, on this of all days. There was of course her mania for cleanliness: a second religion, attended by a fervor that rivaled her love of Jesus. But she seemed to suffer so; the day was supposed to be spent in prayer and reflection of Christ's agony to the exclusion of any other activity. And here she was, bent over a large steaming wooden tub, scrubbing away, frantic as a criminal about to be apprehended at any moment. The sea breeze blew and rocked his hammock and Don Juan could see his daughters ringed around the tub assisting their mother: little Gracia who was ten, and Maria a year younger, standing on boxes so they could reach over the rim and into the tub, and Luisa who was almost a young woman; the three girls worked with great haste wringing water from various garments, hurrying to complete this task so that their mother might commence her day of prayer and devotion. From time to time Doña Gara and the girls glanced fearfully at the walls, the door, and the steaming water to see if Christ's accusatory blood had appeared, marking their sin. The chore of washing went drearily on and on. Don Juan leaning out of the hammock could not help himself and laughed ruefully at such suffering. The hour progressed; Doña Gara knelt on the stone doorstep and pounded the wet wash, glancing over her shoulder, the radio on that day not playing music but groaning Jesus's passion. Jesus staggered to Golgotha; the lash cracked in the air, the wash thumped on the doorstep: Don Juan's eyes growing big with horror, he pointed to the white-washed wall of the house and called, "Look, look!" Doña Gara put her trembling hand to her mouth and stared at the wall where the indictment of the savior's blood did not appear. Don Juan laughed so hard he fell out of the hammock. He lay face down on the pungent earth and heard his wife call, "*Mi cruz, mi cruz.*" Yes, he thought that is how she has named me, "my cross." He arose from the ground declaiming, "Religion is the opiate of the masses." He walked to the open window, wagged his finger at his daughters who were on their knees praying and shouted again, "Religion is the opiate of the masses."

Doña Gara pounded the wash on the doorstep. Don Juan turned from his three daughters on their knees and looked around the room. The two little ones, Carlitos and Margarita, aged five and six, peeked from the bedroom, suppressing laughter; they were, he knew, of his humor. On the shelf affixed to the wall was the small square wooden radio. The dial of the radio had the subdued glow of a captive shrunken sun, upon which the precise and magical markings designating a point of communication were tuned to the lamentations of Mary Magdalene and the wailing of the other Mary. From inside the animated wooden box a mob howled, thunder thundered, and the two criminals crucified along with Christ, harangued the Rabbi nailed between them. They said if Jesus was who he said he was, why not just climb down from the cross. Despite the jeering tone of the crucified criminals Don Juan heard a comradely humor, a rough fellowship of the crucified, and agreed, *si*, why not climb down from the cross; besides, Juan reasoned that his attitude toward Jesus could be no less ruthless than it would be to any rival for his wife's affections. From the little radio he heard the bowels of the earth crack and rumble, and angelic voices rising in a wordless hymn of contrition: the wash thumped on the doorstep and Don Juan grew pensive. That morning, as every morning, coming out from sleep, Doña Gara was the first living thing he saw. Her black hair was streaked with gray and there was the recurring shock of her beauty. Beyond anything they willed he felt how the shapes of their bodies had accommodated one another in sleep. It occurred to Juan that perhaps such beauty had to find its service. He saw her face, neck, her hand under the scallop-edged lace of her sleeve lying on the cover, one coffee colored foot sticking out beyond the hem of her white nightgown and the bed clothes. After twelve years of marriage and nine surviving children this was as much as he ever saw of her. She insisted on this, and the dark. He thought that perhaps the small gnawing at the edge of his heart would stop, if in denying him she had kept her woman's mystery for herself, but it was not for herself, it was for the preeminent Jewish ghost whose earthly administrators were Titi-Tapon, and the priest, sycophant friend of the rich, who also wore black and was fat as a graveyard worm.

Now as Don Juan journeyed from one past to another, his shoeless foot pried at the foot still wearing a shoe; he heard the couch creak, and he thought that the bedroom where he and Doña Gara had slept, with its crucifix, altar, votive candles and representations of Christ's bleeding heart and weeping Mary was not unlike the funeral parlor where he first met the widow Milagro. Milagro's husband, painted and powdered, the face stuffed cherubic with paraffin, lay stretched in his box. Don Juan's drunkard of a brother Toto, sipped rum, eyed the widow's rounded hip, and sang under his breath the old rhumba, "Ay, who is going to fill the void, who is going to fill the void?" Don Juan lay next to Doña Gara in a time that preceded his knowing Milagro and remembered sadly that he had not filled that void. Snug within the dark warmth of Doña Gara's body he sniffed the incense reeking dark at his nose. The heat of her body, her womanly shape in repose under the cover conspired with the invincible presence of how it was when they first touched and he had not felt any rancor in relinquishing command over his spirit and nerves; and even within the first hour of that miraculous time he began to suspect that he would pass through her life only to help her invent her virtue. Don Juan got up out of bed, pushed aside the thick curtain that hung in the doorway and walked out into Good Friday morning. The radio squawked and Doña Gara's savior gave up a final plaintive cry to his father; in the distance Don Juan heard gunshots that sounded like corks popping from wine bottles. Doña Gara, Luisa, Gracia, and Maria, holding in their outstretched arms soaking articles of clothing and dripping wet bedsheets trudged out the rear door of the house to hang the wash to dry. The heat of the sun made sweat run down Don Juan's bent back, while his head thrust through the open window into the kitchen enjoyed cool weather. Carlitos and Margarita moved stealthily from the bedroom to the kitchen and ran in a circle around the wooden tub; they stopped suddenly and smiled at their father. Don Juan with his head and shoulders inside the house, and the rest of him outside, shrugged. The radio sputtered and gagged, the orange light of the dial faded, and the radio was silent. It was then, on the dirt floor, beneath the shelf supporting the radio that Don Juan saw the dark red butterfly oozing a small puddle of blood. Don Juan went quickly into the house and bent down to examine the strange bleeding butterfly and saw that it was a large red ribbon leaking its dye. Even before he was crouched, balanced on his haunches, he knew he would do it, and with a finger pressed to his lips, stifling his nearly irrepressible laughter, he admonished Carlitos and Margarita to do the same. The two children, hands over their mouths, ran to the bedroom, taking their muffled laughter under the bed, where they had a concealed and fine view of the kitchen. Don Juan stood up and squeezed from the wet ribbon three thick drops that ran and stained the white wall with the rusted brown red of sweated blood. He then dropped the ribbon in the tub of water, where there were still several pieces of clothing; he put his hand in and stirred the water until it was blood red. The repressed laughter snorting through his nose, he tip-toed out of the house, dashed to his hammock, climbed in, and stuffed his mouth with his sleeve. Gagging on laughter, he waited. The salt air crept under his shirt and tickled his sweat-lathered back. Suspended above ground in the hammock swaying slightly, teeth clamped on the cuff of his sleeve, and his breath held in suspension, he might have been swimming under the sea, where buoyant and waiting, he saw through the pulsing lights of his squeezed-shut eyes Doña Gara enter the kitchen, look at the stained wall, and the tub of water turned to blood, scream, and fall on her knees. Don Juan lifted his head, opened his mouth and indulged in breath. He could, as Doña Gara could, after the years of marriage, (even while both claimed the impossibility of understanding the other sex, which must have been invented on some alien planet) predict, almost invariably what the other would say or do next. Don Juan waited and nothing happened. He thought that after all, perhaps she had entered the kitchen, seen and known that it was a joke. He peeked out of the hammock and saw Carlitos run out of the door waving his arms and ducking behind the side of the house. Don Juan was ready to silently mouth Doña Gara's exclaiming, "*Sangre de Cristo, O Dios Mio*," but Doña Gara's scream was so awful that after he unplugged his ears he had to resolve not to have remorse. He heard Maria, Luisa, and Gracia crying. He knew that they were on their knees, counting their beads and praying. He considered that it might be just the moment to teach them once and for all that religion was the opiate of the masses.

Doña Gara appeared in the doorway, hobbling on her knees, arms outstretched in the attitude of crucifixion; Don Juan saw on her upturned sorrowful face such unheard-of love and unqualified devotion, that he could feel his own heart contract and burst into a burning ball of gas; he choked and his eyes smarted. For such faithlessness he was tempted to beat her, but he was not that kind of hero. Besides, on her bleeding knees Doña Gara had already progressed halfway up the stone path; she would turn into the patio and continue on her knees, out to the dusty rock-strewn road and on up the six miles, on her knees into the mountains, to the shrine of Our Lady of Perpetual Succor.

Of the five children who were at home four were weeping in the doorway. The fifth, Carlitos, ran from the side of the house, waved the red ribbon and shouted at the stunted form of his mother staggering into the horizon. Doña Gara, on her knees, outstretched arms pinioned in the air, swayed and trembled like an ill-made sail, and Carlitos shouted that it was a ribbon, "only Luisa's ribbon." The other children, in chorus picked up the cry, "only a ribbon, a ribbon," which the wind took and reduced to the remote percussive sound of a bird hammering in a tree, and Don Juan tried to muster the laugh locked in his aching chest.

The weight of Don Juan's eyelids, shut on the brilliant colors of the Island were reluctant to open. Making an effort to rouse himself from the dream, Don Juan knew he must first awaken Angelito, comfortably asleep on his grandfather's lap, within his grandfather's dream. Somewhere inside himself Don Juan heard himself say wake up; but the words only droned into the remembrance of awakening in the little hut Doña Gara had built for him when she returned from the pilgrimage to the shrine of Our Lady of Perpetual Succor. Titi-Tapon had assisted in the building of the hut. It had a tin roof and it took the women one week to complete the project. Don Juan marveled at the soundness of the structure; it was made of wood with two windows, one facing the mountain and the other, the sea. The hut, built on a sloping hill, was on a parallel line, thirty feet below the main house. Doña Gara and Titi-Tapon rigged up a long pole and a system of rope pulleys so that a shelf could ride down from the main house transporting meals to the seaside window of Don Juan's hut. It was Titi-Tapon who delivered the message, inside the freshly whitewashed hut, with Don Juan's hammock strung up so that he could reach from the hammock out the window to the shelf for his morning coffee. Titi-Tapon appearing quite neutral except for a fatalistic sigh, said that her sister la Doña Gara had said that the time of her sharing a bed with Don Juan was over.

Living in the hut was not unpleasant. Doña Gara kept it clean, the meals that rode on the shelf to his window arrived promptly and were often elaborate; on the same shelf fresh linen arrived. After that there was Consuelo.

Don Juan opened one eyelid a crack upon a murk which revealed nothing; he heard a police siren and did not know whether it was the last of the night, or the first of the morning. Doña Gara's voice, the voice of the very old Gara called from far away, "I'll see you soon, you'll like it here; it is not too hot, and not too cold." Again Don Juan protested, saying that he felt fine, and that he was planning on being married that very day.

A moment before the first light he awoke with a slightly nauseous feeling and a pain in his chest, that his face, even in the dark would not acknowledge, since from some concealed place, he knew that Doña Gara was watching. He had slept through the night in his clothes and wearing one shoe. Slowly he slid his stiff legs to the floor, his five toes protruding from his torn sock wriggled and searched, and found the soft backed broken shoe. The dark of the window had faded to a smoky sulfurous yellow. He stood for a while letting his numb legs awaken, and then shuffled a furrow through the ankle-deep wall-to-wall newspaper to a small card table where he kept the provisions for the principal meal of his day. The recipe for Don Juan's broth, which he pronounced "brosh," was always the same. After the broth, he knew he would gain strength; the queasiness in his stomach would go away, and the tightness in his chest ease. He poured three thick drops of evaporated milk from a can into a deep soup bowl and opened a can of Campbell's vegetable soup and poured half of it into the bowl; then he reached for the pint bottle of Bacardi rum and poured half of it into the bowl. He stirred the broth around with his finger, lifted the bowl to his mouth, and in three sets of four gulps, (with a substantial pause after each four gulps) drained the bowl.

The magic began. Lights danced in front of his eyes, the small fire in his belly made the nausea a minor sensation. The tightness in his chest eased a little. Between painful heart beats he was able to say to the man he admired most (after Samuel Gompers) "Jean Valjean, I don't give a damn shit." Don Juan said this, glancing in the direction of the ragged tome of *Les Misérables* leaning toward the edge of the shelf. He lifted the bottle of rum to his mouth and took a long swallow. Dormant armies moved in his blood, liver, and lights, fighting the long betrayal of his body. "*Si, si,*" said Don Juan again, "I don't give a damn shit," preparing himself for adventure; and he thought not giving a damn shit is not so beautiful as Jean Valjean who had to risk being betrayed by revealing his own prodigious strength; and so revealed Jean Valjean would be returned to prison. "But not giving a damn shit is a strength I have when I have it," Don Juan said, thinking that his life-long friend Jean Valjean would understand. Out of the smoky light shining in the window an iceberg burgeoned out of the air and seemed about to crash through the window. Don Juan shuffled to the window and looked out. Nothing moved in the nearly opaque air, and what had appeared to be an iceberg was now a herd of filthy palpable clouds, stagnant and motionless five stories above the street. Outside, on the rotting windowsill, one derelict pigeon roosted headless against the pane; its head was tucked beneath a wing and it looked like an ill-used and discarded toy. Don Juan moved from the window to the card table and slowly, laboriously, bent down beneath the table and turned on the old small wooden radio. The radio squeaked and a pleasant voice announced that it was eight forty-five, the first day of summer, and that the air in the city had been designated as unacceptable; persons suffering from lung and heart ailments were advised to stay indoors. Then there were violins. Don Juan went to the sink with its one rusted faucet and dabbed several drops of water on his cheeks, sprinkled and patted down his hair. He decided not to take his machete, since wearing the weapon at the marriage ceremony would appear odd and unseemly, even if it was only a civil ceremony to take place at city hall. He unlocked the top and bottom door locks, then slipped the chain free and moved to take down the long metal pole that would hold the door in place even if the other locks were jimmied.

Don Juan grabbed hold of the pole from the bottom and yanked, the pole remained fixed in its place. He put his shoulder to the center of the pole, which was angled down to the floor and pushed. The pole scraped several inches along the floor and within the two inches he could maneuver the pole back and forth, but it would not come free. He sweated and there was pain down the length of his right arm. He lifted his left leg, kicked at the pole, and fell backward in a sitting position.

He sat for a while gasping for breath. After he had rested, Don Juan realized that all the while he wrestled with the iron pole he had been struggling to the rhythm of the inane and cloyingly sweet music coming from the radio. He tried to get up but was too tired, and rested for several more minutes. His left hand buried in the turf of crumbling newspapers brought out a yellow fragment of front page that announced that the famous bank robber Willy Sutton had escaped from prison. There was a picture of Dapper Willy with his pencil thin mustache and double-breasted suit, smiling. The date partially torn away read, nineteen fifty something. Don Juan, rising from the floor, shouted "Viva Willy Sutton." He moved to the table where his machete lay, picked it up, bent low, and swung hard beneath the table, cleaving the radio in two. Glass tubes exploded and the sound of violins died away. He then considered going out the window and climbing down the five flights of the fire escape, but he remembered that even if he did not slip and fall, or was not mistaken for a burglar, there was a one-story drop to the sidewalk where the fire escape ended. Don Juan groaned, he was to have met Generosa in Tompkins Square Park at nine-thirty. He reckoned that he was already late, reached for the bottle of rum, took two more long pulls from the nearly empty bottle, and contemplated his escape. Holding the machete in his hand he wondered if the blade were strong enough to cut through the metal sheeted door. He narrowed his eyes, concentrating on the expanse of shiny metal, raised the machete above his head, cried, "Viva Willy Sutton" and charged the door.

When the factory whistle from somewhere along the East River blew to signal the noon hour, Don Juan lay on the floor clutching his machete steadfastly and ignored the pain in his chest. He stared through the jagged hole he had chopped in the door. The hole, just large enough for him to crawl through, was rimmed with teeth of splintered wood and sheet metal. He waited, gathering the necessary strength and nerve to squeeze through the hole that looked like the mouth of a meat-eating animal. It occurred to Don Juan as he lay resting, that his lifelong admiration for Victor Hugo's *Les Misérables* (wherein was depicted Jean Valjean's heroic escape from prison) had somehow created a debt which he was now paying. He honored the debt and studied the door with its jagged hole of dark. His eyes drifted to the door's two metal hinges, and Don Juan thought how much easier it would have been to just unscrew the screws and remove the door. Also he thought of Generosa, of her skin, her lovely hands, and the desire to touch her was so strong that he was willing to inflict any kind of mayhem on this building and humanity, just to be in proximity of her flesh. He rose slowly from the floor, his bones creaked and as he rose his back hit the metal pole, jammed into the door at right angles; it popped loose and clanged to the floor.

Don Juan opened the door and stepped into the darkness of the hallway. He was still clutching the machete in his left hand and thought, for in case, and hung the weapon from his neck by the leather necklace, which was strung through the wooden handle. The tightness at the center of his chest radiated throughout his torso, he could taste the sweat running into his mouth, and there was a chill in his back. He went down the steps slowly; right foot down, then left foot joining right foot, then left foot down. After descending two flights a door opened a thin crack of light, and Don Juan could feel someone studying him as he passed. He continued on his way without altering his pace and did not turn or look behind him.

The journey to the street seemed to take very long, and he thought of Generosa in a white summer dress. He remembered a remark of Gracia, or was it Maria? After seeing Generosa in the white dress one or both had said, "*La Cubana* looks like a fly in a glass of milk," and he thought, they are of *café-con-leche* color themselves. His foot bumped something on the landing: he strained to see and then stepped carefully to avoid the sodden bag of garbage dripping coffee grounds, eggshells, and liquid mess. When he knew he was only two flights from the street Don Juan paused to rest.

The shriek echoed through the hallway and what was left of the hair on his body shivered alive; his heart jumped. He stood still in the thick dimness and concentrated his hearing until the scream and the echo of the scream which had sent maggoty swarms of itching all over his body ceased. Slowly Don Juan reached for the machete. A burning ran the length of his arm. He stabbed at the dark. The dark breathed inhumanly all around him; a strangled exhalation of breath whined near his ear, and as Don Juan turned he hoped that the junkie was as near ruin as he: lifting the machete once more Don Juan felt he must be borrowing strength from a future life and slashed at the dark. The shape of menace beyond the swish of the blade whimpered and shrieked "Marro-own." A small dog ran by Don Juan's feet, barking. From above its unseen master called, "I live a dis building for forty years—you live a dis building?" Don Juan heard the trembling in the voice, and then the trembling in his own, as he answered, "I am not a criminal, you may pass." The man above ventured down several steps, and Don Juan was able to make out the silhouette of someone bent over, and leaning on a cane. "I am Señor Giuseppe Tortini." "I am Don Juan Olivera de Obregon." Señor Tortini did not come closer. Don Juan thought Señor Tortini could see the machete and still suffered uncertainty. Don Juan said, "I am not a criminal, truly you may pass." The other did not pass and said, "After you, Señor."

The faraway voice of above falling down the distance of two flights narrowed and grew small, clear, and as intimate as someone speaking at his ear. "Señor, the blessed Saint Augustine says that the love of a human being, however constant in loving and returning love, perishes, while he who loves God never loses a friend. How long you live a dis building?"

Don Juan moved through the narrow hallway, leaning against the wall, the machete dangled from his hanging arm; now he lacked the breath to answer, although he heard within himself the faint reflexive reply, "opiate of the masses." He could see at the end of the long dark hallway, the open door, a patch of smoky yellow street, and three, perhaps four, figures. From somewhere in the hallway Mr. Tortini's small dog barked. Don Juan thought, *perdoname* Señor Tortini, I don't give a damn, you may have any opiate you wish, I wish the opiate of the female hair of Generosa.

He could not feel his legs anymore, although he was still moving. The weight of the machete felt tremendous and he let go and heard the weapon clatter behind him. Inching along the wall he progressed slowly toward the door and the street. The fetid yellowish fog, smoked in the doorway and everyone was crying. Titi-Tapon and Generosa argued, tears running down their cheeks. At the curb a policeman haranguing an ice cream vendor cried and the ice cream vendor showing his teeth to the policeman, cried. The acrid air stung Don Juan's eyes and he could feel the wetness swell in his eyes and drip down the sides of his face. Generosa turned from Titi. Her black hair had been dyed the color of copper, and her brown skin was luminous in a white dress. She flicked a tear from her eye with a red lacquered fingernail, laughed, and said, "Don't cry, old man," lifting her hand with a diamond ring on one wiggling finger to Don Juan's nose. "Busch's credit *joyeria*," she said, and explained in a hoarse whisper that Don Juan had eighteen months to two years to pay for the ring. She slipped the small booklet with the eighteen stubs for installment payments into Don Juan's trouser pocket. The feel of her hand on his thigh was not nearly so great a pleasure as the thought of the responsibility projecting him eighteen months into the future. The painful constraint of his chest and the ache in his heart had eased. He felt himself suspended in some vast tenderness, and did not understand why Generosa's gravelly voice cooed, "Smile, old man, be happy," certainly he wept for the same reason they all wept. He remembered, the velvety voice of the radio had announced that the air was unacceptable; and Titi-Tapon, wearing a white surgical mask over her nose and mouth to protect herself from the unacceptable air, swung a paper shopping bag from one hand and with the other tugged Generosa's white sleeve as she recited Don Juan's awful history. Generosa nudged him in the ribs with her elbow, and told him the joke about the honeymoon of the ninety-eight-year-old man and sixteen-year-old girl. Generosa said it took the mortician a week to wipe the smile from the old man's face, laughed, and slapped her thighs. Don Juan did not feel himself falling so much as descending into an enormous rapture, his back rode down the hallway wall; looking up, he saw the underside of Generosa's white sheathed bosom, breathing hillocks of infinite promise. Titi-Tapon's voice droned on somewhere above his head: the voice, articulated on an endless sigh, said that that very morning she, Titi-Tapon Doña Gregoria, had restored Don Juan's daughter—who was also her sister—to speech; she (Titi) had given Chaga an enema and Chaga was then able to say good-morning to the mailman. Don Juan looked up the great distance into the valley between Generosa's bosom to the slope of her throat and the underside of her chin and studied the tawny skin of heaven. He could hear beyond the doorway the commotion in the street between the policeman and the unlicensed vendor. The sight of the weeping policeman had touched something in Don Juan and now he wondered at his sudden fledgling compassion for the absurd Inspector Javert, who had hounded Jean Valjean for the theft of a loaf of bread; ridiculous Inspector Javert, who had taken his passion for law to sleep with the fishes. Don Juan, looking through the water in his eyes, could not see clearly, but he knew that the hands removing his shoes from his feet were Titi's.

A Trip

The college set in the Garden of Eden. The nude volleyball players drenched in twilight. Adam and Eve buoyant in the amber air float among the butterflies and the sublime bodies. Their radiant pubic hair, heliotropic bouquets, tug them aloft, where the young men and women drift near the green net, their supple bodies shaped like clef notes of music only they can hear.

How did I get here? I was inspired. I was talking. They gave me drink as long as I kept talking. I talked about books I loved. One young man leaned over the bar and wrote down the things I was saying. A young woman next to him laughed and applauded. She hugged me. I forgot what I was going to say next. Another bought me a drink. I gulped it down and asked for a chaser. They didn't mind. One of the young men shouted to the bartender, "Beer." I lost the thread of what I'd been saying. The young man who had called for the bartender handed the beer to me and said, "Lawrence and Dostoyevsky." I took a swallow and continued to speak. That was in the city, four, no five years ago; my daughter Maria was not yet born.

Now they pay me for it. Talking about books. Fantastic employment.

I wonder, are the students infatuated by my words, or the spectacle of my infatuation? A pied piper susceptible as the children in his wake. They surround me. Demand the secrets of my heart laid bare. I remember when my wife Laura suggested that I get the necessary credentials that would allow an institution of higher learning to recompense me with a salary. I recall the day we talked about it. The newspapers, the television, and the radio were full of the news of the day. Dozens of young people had gone to the floor of the stock exchange and set money on fire. They touched flaming matches to currency, danced and exhorted the herd of stunned traders to join them in dancing and torching money.

Now the young people I speak to are sweetly adamant. When I first arrived from the city, lugging my suitcase across the meadow, and stumbled onto the nude volleyball game, I had a vision out of H. G. Wells' *Time Machine.* The nude college students floating in the paradisal dusk were the lovely and hapless Eloi, and at any moment, the Morlocks, the devolved industrial masses, the kin I fled, would emerge out of a smoking trench and carry off the beautiful people and make a meal of them. But it's not like that at all. I, who first presented subjects to them, have become the subject. It is possible, they insist, to bring about a world ruled by love rather than money, and my participation requires a confession.

They believe in spontaneity. I don't remember everything. They visit our home at odd hours, as they are moved. The accounts of what they say I did conform to the parts I can remember, and the evidence on my body.

Rainbow Schwartz looks like a goofy John the Baptist in his loincloth, planted on his bare reptilian feet. Rainbow offers an exhausted smile. He's barely survived the ravages of his laughter. Laura, my beautiful wife, precipitates intoxication from which I have no desire to recover. She whispers in my ear, "I can't go on living like this, where the hell were you? You've been gone three days." She turns to the roly-poly bald Bible salesman who, in his green suit, white shirt, and red bowtie looks like a defrocked and shorn Santa Claus. Laura points to the front door and says, "Go. Now!" Santa, rosy and jubilant, had been recounting how the "Israelites smote the Arabs in the Six-Day War" which meant, he said, "soon the graves will give up their dead, the sky rain blood, and Jesus will be just around the corner." Maria, my daughter, a week from her sixth birthday had opened the door and saw a beaming Santa toting the suitcase of black Bibles. Maria returned to building a vessel out of blocks. Santa asked "Noah's Ark?" "A spaceship," said Maria, "so the extraterrestrials and my cousins can go someplace nice." Laura, turned to Santa, pointed to the front door and said "Go."

Santa waddled, the momentum of his suitcase of Bibles propelling him to the door.

I wanted to tell Laura that I agree, we should move out of the village, find a place we can rent not so close to campus, a home that cannot be mistaken for part of the college. Laura has been more than hospitable to the students who have found their way to our door. It all began as something festive, an inaugural we will understand some day, say the students. Bernard Tummelman, the brilliant English major, piano and mathematics prodigy, cannot abide Rainbow Schwartz. Tummelman, tall, pale, and tubercular-looking, wears a white shirt, blue tie, and a tweed jacket. He regards Rainbow, trussed in his loincloth, with contempt. Bernard, on the first day of the semester, during the first hour, judged Rainbow as a mere life stylist. Bernard considers the attention I give Rainbow evidence of a serious weakness of my character. Rainbow Schwartz is taking up Bernard's valuable time. Bernard takes Rainbow in obliquely and keeps a couple of yards distant. Were he any closer, Bernard would be in danger of contagion from whatever orthodoxy animates Rainbow's life. Bernard had come to discuss the play he has written. Just before Laura banished Santa, Bernard the explainer, who must be weaned from the explanations that encumber his work, had begun to explain his play. Two commercial travelers, Kafka's Gregor Samsa, a beetle who has given up trying to get a pair of trousers onto his many wriggling legs, and Arthur Miller's Willie Loman, who sustains a lament through convulsive sighs, commiserate with one another in a tolerable suburb of Hell.

Ms. Kim is also waiting. It seems that our class discussion of Tolstoy's *The Death of Ivan Ilych* has precipitated a family crisis. She had begun her undergraduate career as an engineering major. The literature course she happened to take with me became the great illicit thing in her life. Enormously gifted, Ms. Kim's success as an engineer could liberate her mother, father, and two sisters from the family grocery store in Bed-Stuy Brooklyn. Ms. Kim's father dreams of the glory and wealth his eloquent daughter, a wizard with sums, would bring to the family. Now her father promises to die of heartbreak. But it was Ms. Kim's contemplation of Ivan Ilych's long death as the richest opportunity for true thought that led Ms. Kim to the damning judgment of her father's life of obedience and drudgery. She ordained her escape which entails changing her major to Comparative Literature and the study of the Russian language. She hopes to render *Anna Karenina* into English truer to the original than the nineteenth-century euphemisms and anglophile absurdities that characterize the translations now available.

Ms. Kim explained to Laura and has repeated to me, that I must telephone her father and dissuade him from coming to the college where he will beg the president of the college to revoke his daughter's scholarship if she persists in abandoning her responsibility to the family. Ms. Kim repeats, and I don't doubt her, that she wants to devote her life to literature. Ms. Kim cried. "Okay, I'll write your dad, telephone if I have to."

Rainbow Schwartz has attempted to return the conversation back to Dostoyevsky. His curiosity is loaded with messianic concern, which drives Bernard Tummelman over the edge. And as happens when Bernard is out of patience, he throws a tantrum, gushing passages he's memorized from Lewis Carroll's *Alice's Adventures in Wonderland* and *Through the Looking Glass*. Rainbow says, "So Prince Myshkin ..." Bernard declaims:

"'Twas brillig, and the slithy toves
Did gyre and gimble in the wabe;
All mimsy were the borogoves,
And the mome raths outgrabe.
Beware the Jabberwock, my son!
The jaws that bite, the claws that catch!"

Rainbow raises his voice to speak above Bernard's recitation. He reminds me that we have been speaking of Prince Myshkin. Rainbow tries to persuade me that I might be that kind of idiot, and reminds me that I'd noted how, in the presence of Dostoyevsky's prince, everyone, all of Russia, is stripped to some nub of conscience. Laura's glance makes Rainbow tremble, but he is tenacious. He wants me to describe again how, in *The Idiot*, Prince Myshkin's truth-telling wrecks the world. This paradigm of necessary destruction Rainbow believes must come before the new world can be created.

Laura says, "Wait, I want to know how he got this," and pulls the sleeveless sweatshirt up from my waist, leaving it gathered around my neck. A breeze feathers the hair on my stomach. Laura's fingertips tickle the scabs outlining the palm tree on my chest, her name, palimpsest among the gnarled roots. Laura, Maria, Rainbow, Bernard, Chancy, Jesse, and Ms. Kim study me. I'm the evidence of something. I remember myself as the man who wanted to say yes. "Well?" Laura says. Rainbow says, "He's a trip." Bernard says, "*Why, if a fish came to me, and told me he was going on a journey, I should say with what porpoise?*" Laura jabs her finger under my heart, "Who did this?" Bernard says, "*You might just as well say that I breathe when I sleep is the same thing as I sleep when I breathe!*" Laura glares at Bernard. Bernard, mouth gaping, is silent. Laura looked to Chancy and repeats, "Where did he get the tattoo?"

Chancy Lonegan, who rarely said more than "wow," "cool," or "bummer," had several days before our journey to the commune in Maine dropped out of my Modern Lit class. During our last conference I tried to explain to Chancy that I didn't know how to evaluate invisible work. I didn't challenge his claim of greater self-knowledge, nor that he'd reconciled the warring beliefs within himself. I tried but couldn't understand what those beliefs were. It had been a long day. It was getting dark, usually at that hour I was home. Chancy looked at me as Jesus must have looked at Pontius Pilate. He was ready to die for my sins. I asked him if he wanted to wind up in Vietnam and get his ass shot off. He shrugged and showed me the palms of his hands. I resisted the impulse to grab Chancy's ears and shake him. His piety angered and frightened me. Couple of weeks before our journey Chancy had been arrested at an anti-war rally and spent three days in jail. Chancy and his classmates were among those challenging the lies the war was predicated on. I must have said something justifying my right to a drink and reached for the bottle in the bottom drawer of my desk. Chancy withdrew a sock from his jacket pocket, then a mushroom from the sock. He brought the mushroom to my lips, a mother spoon-feeding a child resistant to proper nourishment. I gulped the mushroom down with a shot of Jameson and argued against martyrdom. "It was," I said, "a form of violence. Consider Chancy, how humanity is infatuated by sanctimonious slaughter." Chancy said, "You okay?" I said, "Yeah," and resisted confessing that I had been drafted and served in Korea. However, when I was shipped to Korea the shooting stopped. I'd been safer in Korea than in neighborhoods I had called home. I wondered why I had to keep my good fortune a secret.

I was obliged to discuss with Chancy what Peter Julius, Chancy's academic advisor had told me. Chancy was on academic probation and in danger of flunking all his classes. He was likely to be suspended, perhaps expelled from the college. I reminded Chancy that he would lose his student deferment and become subject to the draft. Peter told me that he'd received an angry phone call from Chancy's dad. He denounced an educational program that allowed his son to focus his attention "on the study of nuts and berries," and slammed the phone down.

The garden Chancy had planted early in the spring semester behind his dormitory yielded lilacs, roses, onions, carrots, and pumpkins. Chancy's husbandry outpaced Vermont's short growing season.

"Chancy, what if I grant you an extension to write the final paper on the topic you chose in response to Anatole France's *The Procurator of Judea?* Did you read it?" "Didn't get to it. What's it about?"

Chancy studied me. I might have represented the temptation to abandon the integrity that had lighted his soul. I might be proselytizing safety. But I had accepted his gift without hesitation, swallowed the mushroom. Maybe that's why his attitude changed—or had Chancy eaten a mushroom before coming to our meeting? The straight-backed wooden chair I sat on was comfortable. Chancy was attentive as a parent listening to his child as an act of good faith. I blundered trying to explain why I was telling him the story. Trying to recover as if from a self-inflicted wound, I said "The story of Pontius Pilate offers a cynical perspective, built on a piddling irony, but consider this, Chancy: here is Pontius Pilate, back in Rome, returned from his duties in Judea. Pilate is being borne by litter bearers. He is on his way to a spa where he hopes the mineral waters will alleviate his gout, fatigue, and ennui. At a juncture on the road where there is a tavern, he gives the order to his slaves to stop. He will dine and rest at the tavern. There he recognizes the tribune.

Pilate is happy to have recognized the old soldier. The tribune's ossified face could belong to another veteran but for the bright blue vigilant eyes.

They talk, drink wine, and reminisce, patriots who endured a pestilential place for the good of their country. They're veterans who share knowledge that cannot be communicated to those who haven't been there. They reiterate, remembering, amazed once more by the backwardness of the place, the stubborn, fanatical people, resistant to any rational improvement. Pilate recalls how his plan to install a hygienic plumbing system, a far-reaching construction of aqueducts that would have done much for the health and civic life of the inhabitants, was resisted by the suspicious natives.

And Pilate, as in the days when they were both young men, chides his former comrade for his impulsiveness. He reminds the old soldier that he could have gone far but for his recklessness, his abandonment of duty to pursue romantic adventures. The old soldier agrees, without rancor, concedes that he did undermine a promising career. Pilate says, "What might have been a brilliant career." Pilate's tone is contrite, as though he were seeking pardon from his old comrade. "But that last episode," Pilate says, "the dereliction of duty when you disappeared to chase after the Jewess, who was after all little more than a prostitute, that incident was looked upon at the highest echelon as too grievous to be mitigated by anything I could say."

The tribune raised his goblet of wine in a salute to Pilate. And Pilate saw himself exonerated in the unerring vision of his old comrade. The accusation that he'd abandoned his comrade had visited Pilate with some regularity. Now absolved, Pilate recalled that when they were young men, they shared confidences, affinities, and aspirations. He was inclined to trust his memories.

Pilate conceded that the tribune's delinquent adventures were no more foolish than his own attempts to govern anarchy. The old soldier noted he needed to clarify something crucial about his history. Mary Magdalene, the Jewess, it could be said that she was a woman of easy virtue. He had heard from comrades whose word he would not dispute that she had sold her favors, but when he knew her she was dancing in the taverns. It was also true that he was mad for the woman; never before, or since, has he been so obsessed. For a time she favored him, and then lost interest. He followed her from tavern to tavern, place to place. When his career, his dignity, struck him as superfluous, once more she cared for him, as if at last he'd shed the accoutrements of the world, and could aspire to enter into an equality with her. However, just as he began to believe in the longevity of their union she disappeared.

The old soldier said he lost his mind entirely. His only one thought was finding her again. Even after the passing of years and infirmities of aging, the desire to see her reigned in his heart.

She'd vanished. He followed rumors. It seems she became a follower of a preacher from Nazareth, followed him and his ragged band of peasant believers. "It seemed I always arrived too late to a remote hamlet or strangely hushed tavern, some pathetic oasis barely worthy of the name. The mordant Jewish peasant lingered, barely able to hide his contempt, ready to tell me, yes tribune, they left a little while ago, to the north, south, east, or west. I followed her. She followed this Jesus. Pilate, do you remember him?"

And Pilate, who wanted to empathize with his old comrade, could, in an intellectual sense, understand the tribune's obsession. He tried to remember, as if his recollection could assuage his friend's longing. "Jesus?" Pilate said, but he couldn't recall. Although he did not want his comrade to think him indifferent, he could not muster the energy to lie. "Jesus?" Pilate said, pausing, searching his memory. "No, I don't remember him."

Chancy said "Wow" and seemed at the point of asking a question but changed his mind.

We were standing in front of the dormitory, where my office was located. The grass covering the tantalizing swell of hill on which I stood was an impossible blue. The sky veiling God's face, lavender, speckled with stars, in one instant winking and blinking, in the next cold, brilliant, and remote. Rainbow Schwartz appeared, shivering like a tuning fork. He came closer.

Chancy, in his earth-spattered overalls looked above, consulting the weather God. I followed Chancy's gaze, saw tumbling clouds and sensed the Creator tossing fate, hurly-burly falling down, the last binge before the end of days, love and every kind of folly in contention. The laughter and cheers of young women from the surrounding dormitories rang in the brilliant dark.

The students were gone. Maria was asleep in her bed upstairs. Laura and I sat at the kitchen table. She poured coffee into our cups and assessed me from far away. I was shaken, wanted to tell her everything. She said, "You were gone three days; where the hell were you?" I pounced on Laura's question as a hopeful sign. It reminded me of our early intimacy, when we shared experiences that happened before we met, things we'd barely believe were happening while they were happening, absurd dreams threatening nightmare. We shared confidences in bed after making love. Telling and retelling the stories in bed or walking the city streets, the stories came closer to full term, and accrued meaning.

Laura, courteous, her empathy circumscribed by objective reckoning, scared me.

"Laura, I remembered our anniversary. I wanted to surprise you. I needed to do something irrevocable. I asked Jesse to do the tattoo. Laura Providencia stitched in my skin, a tribute to my love and the sunlit island of your birth. That's why I asked for the palm tree and your name in the vicinity of my heart."

Laura studied me. What I hadn't said, what I didn't know I knew, came like an accusation. Laura Providencia indelible in my flesh was also an aspect of a necessary transgression, a prerequisite for a larger embrace. As a vestigial Jew I felt myself challenging a hoary edict damning graven images.

Laura said "That's a mouthful." She wouldn't let me hold her hand. I said "Please listen." She said, "I'm listening." Laura had described herself as a lapsed Catholic. Still, she prayed and lit candles. I wondered if her listening to me was a priestly function. I wanted to tell her everything I remember.

The headlights of the lollipop-orange Volkswagen bus illumined the prophetic dark. I was a passenger. I'm not sure why. Under the influence I was compelled to follow through with the act that was beyond doubt a moral imperative.

The inside of the vehicle commodious as a Bedouin prince's tent, I sat on a mattress, madras sheets breathing an enclosure. I could see through the draped folds the back of Chancy's head. He was at the wheel. Rainbow sat in the passenger seat beside him. Jesse was stretched out on pillows next to me, resting his head on an olive-drab duffle bag. Rainbow shouted, "Wow!" The shit in Jesse's duffle bag—take three tokes and your hidden desires, secret practices, can be shouted from the rooftops. Nothin's shameful, nothin's gotta be secret."

I saw over Rainbow's shoulder through the windshield the vehicle's headlights penetrating the mist. A sign floated by that said, "Peru." Jesse opened one eye and said, "You shoulda taken the roundabout in Paris." I recalled rural advice to the lost. "You can't get there from here." Chancy said, "We'll get there when we get there." Jesse said, "I got clientele waitin' on me." Where, I wondered was there. Wherever it was I needed to get to a bus depot, return home. I searched my pockets, found nine dollars and some change. How much would the fare home cost? I could borrow the money I needed, but we were lost, it was snowing, the road slippery, progress hypothetical.

We arrived in the dark. Two young men and a young woman ushered us out of the bus. They welcomed Jesse with hugs, Rainbow, Chancy, and me with fraught hellos. One of the young men said, "I'm Tom; when we get you settled we'll have tea." The other young man swallowed a yawn and expelled his name as if it were an impediment. I wondered if he'd said "our" or "hour." The young woman wearing a peacoat and beret handed a flashlight to Jesse, introduced herself as Maxine, said, "That way." She joined Tom and the sleepy young man she identified as Art, aiming the beams of their flashlights on the glazed white ground, diagramming the road we would follow. The slush underfoot made each step forward tentative. The wind bellied transparencies in the curtain of snow and rain. Maxine said, "We don't have far to go." Inside the house two wood-burning stoves, one on each end of a room about the length and width of a double-wide trailer, warmed the place. The bunk beds were comfortable.

The morning was bright, not especially cold. The slush froze into bumpy terrain. We walked slowly. Maxine walked ahead of us and pointed at the barn that had been refurbished into a dining hall. Chancy followed Maxine. Rainbow walked at my side, proselytizing. He tried to persuade me to sample Jesse's revelatory weed. I put the joint in my jacket pocket. Rainbow explained that Jesse wasn't all about business. He was a Vietnam vet and he had joined Rainbow, Chancy, and others from their dormitory at the anti-war rally. "Jesse's passion," said Rainbow, "is truth."

The dining hall was cavernous. Voices echoed. Many tables and chairs. We walked among the commune people down an aisle between two counters and helped ourselves to silverware, plates, and food. At the entryway adjacent to the hall that led to the dining room was the kitchen. Two feet below the ceiling, daylight flowed through a series of horizontal windows. On every table a hurricane lamp. I sat at a table not far from where Jesse and Chancy sat listening to two commune residents. I overheard a good part of what was being said. Chancy nodded yes as if confirming the validity of what he'd heard. Jesse said, "Okay, it's gonna be all right," and patted the shoulders of the young man and young woman who had told them what had happened the previous day.

Rainbow had joined me for breakfast and left following a woman who was about to move a flock of sheep out of a paddock into a loafing shed. He'd volunteered to move bales of hay.

Chancy walked to my table, sat down, and asked a question I didn't hear. "Professor," he said, "are you there?" It was not like Chancy to be sarcastic. My attention wandered. I knew part of the story I'd overheard during Jesse and Chancy's conversation with the two commune people. Chancy commenced a summary of the story he'd told while I had been preoccupied with how I could make amends to Laura. Perhaps the story Chancy was telling was retribution for my rendering of *The Procurator of Judea*.

In the entryway to the dining hall there was a phone booth. I considered phoning Laura. But when I found myself rehearsing what I might say to her I was ashamed.

Chancy said, "Jesse asked me to ask you to please be there. I gotta a job of work to do, the guy who does the plumbing needs help. Are you gonna go or not?" "Where?" "Over there, the other side of the dining hall, near the exit."

The tables and chairs were arranged in a circle that accommodated twenty people including Jesse and me. I heard versions of what had happened the day before we arrived. A young man suggested that if the hunters returned, they could be invited to join a discussion that could raise the consciousness of us all. Some commune people groaned, others tolerated what they heard in silence. Another commune member suggested alerting the sheriff to what had happened. She was reminded that the sheriff like the constable was antagonistic to the commune. If the law found pot or seeds, that could be a pretext for closing the commune. A woman spoke of the need to sustain participatory democracy whatever the difficulty. An aged man, white hair hanging to his shoulders and wearing a bathrobe, stood at an invisible lectern, his hands caressing the air. He explained that the present confluence of events was composed of Jungian synchronicity and Marxist dialectic that could not be made plain by any shuffling of a Tarot deck. "Losing a night's sleep over this will accomplish nothing. Good night, dear ones."

I was about to leave. Some folks were fidgeting in their seats. The person sitting next to Jesse rose from a chair and walked to the center of the gathered community. There was brief applause. Someone shouted, "Debbie, tell it like it is." Debbie stood still, did not say a word until the chatter ceased and everyone was seated. Debbie? Could this be the Deborah Chancy had been telling me about, the sculptor and potter whose work was available at prestigious galleries in New York? Chancy said that Deborah's pots and statues provided most of the revenue that kept the commune afloat. Deborah and Jesse shared a long and significant history. Once upon a time they might have been a couple. The sight of Deborah was unsettling. She could have been thirty or forty. She wore a gray smock, a baseball cap and work shoes. Her handsome face revealed only what she chose to disclose. The fluency of her misshapen hands made art out of clay, stone, and metal.

Deborah described what was seen and thought, despite her being in New York, taking care of business when the hunters intruded. She did not suggest a remedy for what had happened or further analysis of why it happened. Deborah's succinct description presented a verity, its modesty like magic. The day before Jesse, Chancy, Rainbow and I arrived, one of the hunters had stumbled upon Mary, at work in the pottery shed. The hunter stank of booze. The hunters were frustrated. The November rain had washed away the snow cover. The New Jersey hunters could not track deer. Mary, friendly even though she disapproved of hunting, and would not eat meat, offered the hunter a cup of tea. The sad hunter separated from his companions had been grumbling about the things in life that ought to be free and uncomplicated. Mary agreed that in an acquisitive, materialistic society we become slaves to false necessities. Mary said she didn't become frightened until he started to touch her, and even as he tugged at her blouse and she struggled to fight him off he continued to mumble his grievances. He was convinced that the impossibility of hunting and his stumbling into the place where free love reigned was portentous, and the hunter couldn't understand why she would single him out for rejection. She screamed and struggled, others from the commune came running at about the same time that the hunter's companions found him. The three drunk, laughing, hunters drove up in a new red Ford station wagon. They carried their struggling friend away, trying to mollify him, "After all," one explained, "who said that life was supposed to be fair?"

The four hunters, wearing iridescent orange jackets and caps, returned. I had been on my way to the building where I slept the previous night. Jesse came up to me, handed me a bottle and said, "Brandy." I had a shot. Jesse had a shot. He said, "I heard you've been in the service." I said, "Yeah." Jesse said, "wait over there behind the pine. I'll be right back."

Jesse handed me the rifle. He carried a shotgun. Deborah, Chancy, and Rainbow were directing people into the dining hall. Jesse, cradling the shotgun, closed the distance between himself and the hunters. They got out of the new red station wagon and started to walk toward the dining hall. Two carried rifles over their shoulders like soldiers on parade. One clenched a bouquet of weeds with the mock seriousness of a man courting. He said to the companion next to him, "candy is dandy but liquor is quicker."

The burning bush was talking to me. I fired believing that I was giving a lesson in empathy as I blew out the headlight of the new red Ford station wagon, clearly the most beloved possession of the hunter marching with his rifle. He crumpled in grief. Jesse raised the barrel of the shotgun into the face of the hunter who appeared to be the leader of the bunch. Jesse said, "Please go, or there's gonna be some new faces in Hell shortly."

Jesse, Chancy, and Rainbow were part of the celebration. I smoked the pipe passed to me. On a shelf below the windows candles in the shape of gnomes, flowers, unicorns, rainbow-colored vulvas and phalluses melted and drooled, glowed and freckled the faces of Buddha and Che Guevara on the wall. I was absolved of the need to reconcile contradictions. The stereo blared "All You Need Is Love." The melody bounced. The dancers leapt, feet tom-tom-ed the floor. Little bellies of flame danced. The next song was "Blowing in the Wind." I would have preferred Jerry Mulligan. I noted that Deborah had not joined the festivity. I sensed from Deborah not a reproach but her distaste for what she deemed gestures of gallantry. Incense filled the air with the scent of lilacs. Rainbow said, "Far out, Professor, you're a trip, like the gunfight at the OK Corral." A couple dancing close by cheered. One young man, dancing alone, throbbing and waving the great fan of his hair, wheezed, "Bad Karma, bad." Jesse working at the tattoo on my chest by the light of a kerosene lamp said, "Honkies messin' with my clientele is unacceptable. I won't have it."

That was all he had to say on the subject. Jesse guided the electric stylus that gnawed at my chest. He dabbed the blood away with a clean cloth and I watched the palm tree with my wife's name take form in my skin. Could it be that after the nightmare of Vietnam, Jesse could only experience interpretation and history as a violation of his being? Jesse was and would be whatever he was doing. Was this the affinity that brought Jesse and Deborah together? I found resemblances in Jesse of Jesse James and Billy the Kid, Jesse shining among the most endearing of American killers. Still, I wanted to reassure the young man who'd said "bad Karma," and any of the others who saw me and Jesse as symptoms of the world's bad news. After all I was over thirty, although not by much. I reminded everyone of the fortuitous thing. Chancy had decided to go to Canada with his new friend Morty the Candlemaker. Morty, a transient resident of the commune, was also in flight from military service. Once again I thought many of these young people, however privileged, whatever their giddy tantrum, were seriously opposing the war. They might succeed in unleashing those forces in American life that could at last bring a halt to the slaughter. Aside from what I found silly, this was also a glorious moment for American democracy.

Polly, the commune's favorite interpreter of the I Ching, a diminutive girl who appeared little more than a child, wearing large horn-rimmed glasses, concentrated her face in a serious look. She read a Tarot deck and said it augured well. Morty and Chancy, the dreamers running away to dream, would be sustained by the candle business which Morty would teach Chancy. Best of all, the stars pointed north, away from the hell of carnage. Chancy's father, a veteran of WWII and believer of doing one's duty without question, would eventually, Polly said, reconcile with his son. Morty could count on continued financial support from his parents as long as he kept a distance from home. I longed for home.

I mentioned that Thanksgiving was less than a week away. Laura explained we wouldn't be having Thanksgiving together.

She said that she had joined an organization. The purpose of the organization, a peer-counseling group, was to offer support and guidance to the families of alcoholics. Wives, husbands, sons, daughters, brothers and sisters, anyone whose life was affected by an alcoholic, was welcome to join. Laura said she and Maria would be having Thanksgiving dinner with their group and that she had attended her first meeting while I was away.

The moment before I was able to speak again was longer than my recent journey. Although I'd seen Laura's exasperation, I'd assumed that our love was as inexhaustible as my delight each morning to open my eyes and see her.

Finally I said that I had never lost a day of work because of drinking and never lost a job. She said, "Not yet." She also said that I was in the binge stage of my drinking career, I hadn't yet hit bottom.

The thought of our life together as an item for therapeutic gossip, the meaning of our marriage matriculating through psychobabble, was a betrayal and degradation I'd never imagined happening to me.

Laura anticipated what I would say next and told me, "You can't be here anyway. Your mother called three times while you were away. I expected you home on Friday and I told her I'd give you the message as soon as you got here. After her second call late Friday night I concocted an excuse, which is something I'll never do again. That's over. Anyway, I said that I was sorry, that I'd forgotten that you had to attend a conference out of town. She didn't believe me and was certain that I was preventing you from answering the telephone. When she called back the third time early Saturday morning, she said that people who dig graves for others often fell in themselves, and before hanging up, ranted in Yiddish, cursing me in ways I'd rather not have translated." I said, "Darling, I'm sorry." Laura said, "She is a frightened old woman. And your Uncle Sol called. He said your mother's behavior has become very strange and that you should come to New York at once. Despite the war that was their marriage, she has never recovered from your father's death. She doesn't cope very well on her own. And your mother had discolorations on her back that her doctor diagnosed as benign. Still, she is certain she's close to death. Uncle Sol said that you are the only one who might be able to persuade her otherwise. And there are other complications. Your Uncle Sol and your Aunt Tessie could not reach your mother at home. They tried phoning and then went to see her. They knocked and no one answered the door. She has been away for a little more than a week, although she telephoned Aunt Tessie and Uncle Sol and left a message for you. No one has any idea where she was calling from. Your Uncle Sol, who helps her balance her checking account, says that she's withdrawn all her savings. Sol called again to say that she returned to her apartment yesterday and was giving all her belongings to neighbors. Sol said that in his last conversation with her she cursed him in Yiddish, which he translated for me as "onions should grow from your navel."

During the eight-hour bus ride to New York I comforted myself with the thought that Laura and I, unable to sleep, had to touch, hold one another, and the touching took us to lovemaking. But at sunup, everything she said, every gesture suggested that the lovemaking may have been Laura's parting gift.

Laura said, "You'll have to take the bus." I asked, "Why?" "The car needs brake work and I'd rather not think of you driving." I remembered that not long ago under the influence, I'd parked the car somewhere and it took several days to find it again. "Laura, I'll cut down on my drinking." "Really! How many times have you made that promise?" "Laura, how are you going to get your paintings to the show in Boston?" "I'll manage."

On the street beneath the elevated train, five blocks from my mother's apartment, the inhabitants of my mother's neighborhood, mostly aged people, were able to make themselves heard, although the sound of the Atlantic Ocean, only one block to my right, was drowned out by the thunder of the trains overhead. My parents had moved to Brighton Beach also known as Little Odessa, a short while after Laura and I had married. The incredible lung power of the old folks seemed a natural endowment, requiring no special effort. The wonderful aroma of baked goods and smoked meat drifted out of the shops and delicatessens lining the street and mixed with the scent of the ocean. The movement of the people in the street was urgent and happy. The congested traffic in the shadow beneath the elevated trains screeched; the expert near misses between cars, taxis, and buses in no way inhibiting the pedestrians. Young or old, nimble or staggering, dodging the vehicles they cursed. There seemed something more festive than usual about the older inhabitants. They lurched, dazed and giddy. I stood holding the compact overnight bag that held the *AA Big Book* Laura had packed with my things. I'd promised her I would read it. The tide of street traffic had swept me between two clusters of old folks. Buffeted among the old bodies I looked over their heads. In the window of the delicatessen

135

a roasting chicken, dripping its juices, turned on a rotisserie, and the old people standing outside moaned like erotic maniacs at a burlesque show. I squeezed myself out of this group, working my way toward the easier flow of traffic, but was momentarily stuck in another knot of old folks standing before a newspaper kiosk. "Did you hear?" someone in the crowd called, "We're innocent!" "Oh yeah," another said, "of what are we innocent?" "We didn't," the chorus chanted, "kill *Gott*." "You don't say?" another said, convulsed with joy. "I do say." I craned my neck and maneuvered to get a little closer to the kiosk. I glimpsed the front page of a newspaper on the counter. The Vatican concluded that the Jewish people should not be declared guilty of deicide. I was bumped out of position by an old gentleman with a cane. The proprietor of the kiosk pointed at me with the stub of his cigar and bawled, "Sonny boy, this ain't a library, you wanna read you gotta spend a dime." Several celebrants were waving newspapers above their heads like flags. A large woman to my left, creating space for herself with her elbows, read aloud that there were priests who objected to the Vatican's decree. The call and response from the east and west of the crowd was "Let them wallow in Hell—in their bones." I wondered, is it possible with Buddhist monks setting themselves on fire, and kids rioting in New York and Paris, that the cry from the streets had reached Rome? "So, *nu?*" a voice from the heart of the crowd cried, "if we didn't kill God, who did?" After a brief pause, someone answered, "Maybe the Puerto Ricans."

I worked my way free of the crowd and before turning left on Brighton Sixth Street to walk the four blocks to my mother's house, stopped at a candy store to buy a pack of cigarettes.

I asked for a pack of Luckies. The wizened old guy behind the counter slapped down the pack of cigarettes, blew his nose into a hankie, and said, "You heard? We didn't do it. So who did it?" I said I didn't know. He said trembling, "Could be the Hungarians, antisemite bastards."

I knocked on my mother's door. No one answered, not a sound from her apartment. I knocked, waited, and called "Ma." An old woman came slowly towards me resting on her chrome walker. She was wrapped in a great quilted robe. "A mother," she called down the narrow hallway, "can wait forever." I said, "I'm sorry." She said, "Everybody is sorry." She paused and rested midway down the corridor. A plastic bag of trash tied with a string hung from her walker. "Come," she commanded, "do a mitzvah." She handed me the bag of garbage and pointed to the incinerator drop at the end of the hall. As I dropped the neatly tied bag down the chute she said, "Your mother's walking on the boardwalk. Such a nice day you should take advantage, *nu*, go." As I pushed the elevator button and waited, the old woman laughed and said, "So you heard the news?" And before she could take me through the paces of the joke, I said, "They say we didn't kill God, maybe it was the Ukrainians." "*Oy*," she said, "such a sage. Go, go find your mother."

The benches in the Brighton Beach section of the boardwalk were loaded with old folks bundled in topcoats sunning themselves. Some held reflectors under their chins. I unbuttoned my coat as I walked, it was quite warm. I studied the benches looking for my mother. Above, the clouds gyrated, the seagulls hung like kites, and the ocean lay calm. The tide was out and the surf gurgled on the shore. I passed a group of four men seated around a card table playing pinochle. A little further on I walked past an old guy in a fur cap singing "Romania, Romania" to an audience of two fur-coated old women seated on a bench, holding parasols above their heads. I walked on past an old guy strolling and serenading himself with a balalaika. It occurred to me that I was lucky that my grandfather had been a draft dodger from the Czar's army and then I wondered what urgent business my mother's fear of death had precipitated, and how I could persuade her that she wasn't about to die. Perhaps she could no longer live alone, unassisted.

By the time I passed the parachute jump, and the Cyclone, Coney Island's notorious roller coaster, both closed for the season, there weren't many strollers on the boardwalk. Despite my casual stride I'd examined all the benches carefully and mistaken one old woman for my mother. She had been ready to embrace me even as I backed away and said, "Oh, excuse me."

I thought that before trying to convince my mother of anything I should show her Maria's latest drawing, which I carried in my inside breast pocket. I would tell Momma how well her granddaughter was doing in kindergarten. The child could already read "*kinehora*." Every utterance of her granddaughter was received as pure genius, the only proof of the miraculous in the otherwise benighted world.

I was thirsty. I remembered that unlike past occasions, before I left, Laura hadn't extracted the promise that I wouldn't drink. This restraint was probably an aspect of the new program she'd committed herself to as a member of the self-help group. I felt relieved and threatened; this was, perhaps, the beginning of something final. But I reasoned that if I had a couple of beers, no hard stuff, that wasn't really drinking. I descended a ramp from the boardwalk into the Coney Island streets, and after walking two blocks found Clancy's Bar and Grill. I would have two, perhaps three beers at most, and then search the boardwalk again, this time walking in the direction of Brighton Beach, and if I didn't see my mother, I'd try her apartment again.

Clancy's Bar and Grill was burrowed in perpetual dusk. The neon beacon in the opaque window said Rheingold. There were five patrons seated in the bar. I pulled up a stool and sat down. The bartender, a huge woman with one of the most beautiful and tranquil faces I'd ever seen, smiled and said, "What will it be?" Looking up at her I was a kid again sitting too close to a movie screen where my vision climbed the larger-than-life head of unbelievable beauty. I said, "Beer." She tilted the glass expertly under the spigot and lowered the beer to me. She rolled as though on coasters to the far end of the bar where a male patron had called, "Maureen." "Jimmy," she said, "you've had enough, it's time to go home," and pushing back the change he'd left on the bar, said, "Hang on to that, don't play the numbers. Pay your insurance premium." Jimmy nodded. "You promise?" Jimmy said, "I do," and made his way to the door with the deliberate gait of a man who must concentrate not to fall.

Maureen studied another patron sipping a mixed drink from a tall glass. The man was dressed in a business suit, shirt, and tie. He was not young. "Arthur," she said, "you should think about having a sandwich before you continue your rounds, and don't forget your briefcase."

Two stout sweating men sitting side by side at the bar, wearing suits, waiting impatiently for the sandwiches they'd ordered, spoke of hunger during the Great Depression. Each one shouted a salvo of the name of a street, avenue, park, that had been a Hooverville. Finally one of the men answered the question his companion had asked before the men had begun shouting commemorations into one another's face. "Yeah, business is OK. I ain't gonna get rich, but the Mrs. and me ain't living in want. Comes the summer we go to the mountains for a week. Stay in a hotel. And how's by you? You set your son-in-law up in business?" "My son-in-law? It took him a year to go bankrupt." "So whatta ya gonna do?" "What can I do? The bum can't even get arrested." Maureen said, "Enough, stop yellin' or take it outside."

Maureen turned to the one woman patron at the bar. The woman, wearing a checkered cloth coat and a kerchief covering a nest of wire curlers, smoked a cigarette and studied the glass of sherry set in front of her. She sat in a cloud of cigarette smoke. I lit one up. She said, "Maureen, he ain't interested. I know we've been married ten years, there's the three kids, and he works the night shift and all. But he's so damned polite, like I'm a stranger and he gotta be somewhere else." Maureen asked, "And who's with the kids now?" "Oh, the sister." I drank my second beer and signaled with the empty glass for a third. Maureen served me and said, "It won't hurt to slow down, fella," and she returned to the woman customer sitting in the cloud of blue cigarette smoke. I imagined Maureen a former maenad, no longer in the employ of Dionysus, domesticated and grown huge in her good works. "Now, Fay," Maureen said, "Your Charlie is devoted to you and the kids. He's a steady provider. Many would consider you a lucky woman." "That," said Fay, "ain't the issue" and tilted over the bar whispering into the white expanse of Maureen's aproned bosom. "Well certainly," Maureen said, "you could try that. After all, you've got a marriage license, and if you feel the need to confess you can do it here." "But," said Fay, "he doesn't find me attractive no more. It's the weight, I think; after all I'm five feet tall and I weigh a hundred and forty pounds." "Oh darlin'," said Maureen, "what's to worry, my ass weighs a hundred and forty pounds."

Outside on the street, at the foot of the steps leading up to the boardwalk, twilight was brighter than the interior twilight of the bar. I guessed that there was about an hour of daylight left. The sky above the ocean was violet, on the horizon a seam of silver glimmered on the blue-black sea. The boardwalk was almost deserted. To my left, here and there lights went on in apartment windows. The wind had picked up, but it was more refreshing than cold. In Vermont, weather this moderate in November would bring snow. The air smelled of rain. I found myself rehashing some of the things I should have said to Laura before I'd left. She'd said with uncharacteristic bitterness that I was sober on the mornings I preserved for writing, but did not grant my relationship to her the same importance. I'd had no answer.

When I reached the Brighton Beach area of the boardwalk the only people left were the four resolute pinochle players still at the table, and one old guy in a folding chair, under a large brimmed slouch hat. He was wrapped in a blanket, snoring, while from the portable radio in his lap a mellifluous voice crooned "Embraceable You." I stopped, rested for a moment, and touched the inside jacket pocket that held my daughter's drawing. I would present this right off to the first woman in my life, who, according to my uncle's reports, was preparing for her imminent death. I tried to light a cigarette. Even with my hands cupped to protect the tiny flame, the breeze extinguished the bit of fire before I could light up. One of the pinochle players, without rising or looking away from his cards, handed me a smoking cigar. I lit my cigarette from the burning end of the cigar, returned it, and said, "Thanks." The pinochle player grunted. The four card players bundled in their coats and hats around the table seemed impervious to the weather, the season, the time of day. Their profound meditation on the cards might have been an esoteric reckoning with which they hoped to fathom God's aliases. From the lap of the sleeping man the portable radio played and I recognized the voice of the young Frank Sinatra. The card players' hands moved, their lips moved, and their eyes moved, as when intrusion of the outside world threatened to impose itself, as I had. An efficient response was necessary to keep any distraction to a minimum. They rarely spoke. Kibitzers would not be tolerated. I inhaled, taking smoke into my lungs; it tasted good, and I was ready to move on.

The one who had given me his cigar to light my cigarette, cocked his eye toward the street side of the boardwalk and moaned, "Oy, it's Irving's Shirley." Another set of eyes surfaced above the rim of the cards he was holding and said, "Who?" "Shirley, Shirley," the other growled, "She ain't coming for me." The third card player, emerging from his meditation, but alert to his surroundings, said, "That ain't Shirley." The fourth card player slid his bifocals up and down his nose. The woman marching toward the card table had her arms spread wide. She was wearing a silver-colored fur coat, or some synthetic that looked like fur, her banana-yellow hair was done up in pageboy fashion, popular I think during World War II. As she bore down on the table, she called, "Yoo-hoo, darling, suppertime," and the pinochle players looked at one another accusingly.

She blundered into me. A powerful aroma of lilac enveloped us and I wasn't certain whether it was the woman's perfume, or the scent unleashed by the mushroom I'd eaten several days before still inhabiting my senses. The woman's arms moved to embrace me. I had backed away from the woman I'd mistaken for my mother, just as she was about to hug me. I felt that maybe if I overcame my squeamishness, was a bit more generous and embraced this woman, surely someone's bereft mother, my own would appear. Her face had the tooled perfection of a doll. Sumptuous, lacquered eyelashes, blue mascara, but under the rouge of both cheeks, there were large bruises. We were in each other's arms. She moaned, "*Oy, mein kind.*" I held her at arm's length and said, "Mrs ..." She said, "Come to supper. I'll make you potato latkes." I said "Sorry, really I don't have time." She said, "Since when don't you have time for potato latkes?" One of the pinochle players mumbled, "Go, go eat the potato latkes." "Did you," she said, "call your brother? Blood is thicker than water, and Jacob hangs on your every word." "Ma?" "Yeah, me," she said. "What have you done?" "My nose I done. And don't worry, the doctor said the bruises will go away in a little while. And I look like Ginger Rogers, no? And the blond hair is also pretty?" I thought I must find a telephone booth and call Laura, tell her everything so that I can believe it's happening. This day nearly as eternal as childhood. "Your brother, he's a poor eater, a boy with problems. If he had a trade, the right girl. But you, you're an eater," she said smiling. I knew the voice. It was my mother's voice coming from the waxworks Ginger Rogers. She was holding my hands, smiling. I tried to smile. Why did she mutilate herself? I thought of noses and how medical quacks had attached leeches to Gogol's nose as he lay on his deathbed. I remembered my mother's rapture over my daughter's pert nose as the most notable accomplishment of my life.

The pinochle mavens hunched over their cards barely glanced at us. In their improvised, monastic retreat, hiding from their mates, they slapped their cards down with the vehemence of children. The sleeper in the folding chair snored, and from the portable radio in his lap Sinatra sang the refrain of "Embraceable You." Momma said, "Come Izzy, like Fred and Ginger, I'll let you lead." The moon was visible although it was not yet night. We waltzed around the table of the card players, the dance as much as I would ever be able to do to convince my mother she is beautiful.

Acknowledgements

My gratitude to Marc Vincenz and his staff for their thoughtful consideration of my work. Anna Herrick's editing and insightful reading of the stories in *Testimony* has been crucial to the creation of this book. I thank Paul Nelson and Lorrie and Barry Goldensohn for continuing my education.

These stories and earlier versions of some stories, previously appear in the following publications:

"The Matinee" from *AGNI* 60 and *Love's Labours* (Fomite, 2012).

"In the Park" and "Exaltation" from *Love's Labours* (Fomite, 2012).

"Testimony" excerpted from "Patricide: A Novella" in *Love's Labours* (Fomite, 2012).

"Far East" and "Abe and Izzy" (originally titled "Saul and Davy") from *Chekhov Was a Doctor* (Zephyr Press, 2005) .

"The Trip" from *Courting Laura Providencia* (Zephyr Press, 2001).

"Don Juan, the Senior Citizen" from *The St. Veronica Gig Stories* (Zephyr Press, 1986).

Excerpt of "Jabberwocky" recited in "The Trip", from *Through the Looking-Glass* by Lewis Carroll, originally published in 1871.

About the Author

JACK PULASKI grew up in the Williamsburg section of Brooklyn, New York. Pulaski's authored two novels: *Courting Laura Providencia* and *Chekhov Was A Doctor*, and two short story collections: *The St. Veronica Gig Stories* and *Love's Labours*. His stories have appeared in *Agni*, *The Iowa Review*, *Ohio Review*, *Ploughshares*, *MSS.*, and *The New England Review*, as well as in two anthologies: *The Pushcart Prize I* and *The Ploughshares Reader*. He is the recipient of fiction awards from the Coordinating Council of Literary Magazines, the Pushcart Prize, and has received the Special Merit Award in the Nelson Algren Short Fiction Contest twice. Pulaski currently resides in Vermont.